FOR EVER AND EVER

Viola felt sick with nerves as she looked up to see the Earl marching towards her. He had barely reached her when, out of nowhere, Millicent appeared with a sulky look on her face.

"Charles, you promised you would dance this one with me," she pleaded in a wheedling tone of voice whilst twirling a curl around her finger.

"I am sorry, Miss Armitage, but you must be mistaken. I have already promised Miss Brookfield the first dance. Viola?" he added, offering her his arm.

Viola felt as if it was a dream as he led her onto the dance floor. Immediately, his strong arms took her in his charge as they swept around in an elegant waltz.

"I confess that I have never seen anyone more lovely than you are tonight," he whispered, as the *Blue Danube* swelled in her ears. "You are so very beautiful. I am breathless with admiration."

Viola lowered her eyes as her heart sang. She moved nearer to him as they danced and it thrilled her to be so close.

'I love him so much,' she thought, as she gazed up into his warm green eyes, 'would it be too much to hope that he might care for me?'

As they swung round, she caught sight of Millicent who was dancing with an elderly gentleman. She shot Viola a look full of vitriol.

THE BARBARA CARTLAND PINK COLLECTION

1. The Cross of Love
2. Love in the Highlands
3. Love Finds the Way
4. The Castle of Love
5. Love is Triumphant
6. Stars in the Sky
7. The Ship of Love
8. A Dangerous Disguise
9. Love Became Theirs
10. Love Drives In
11. Sailing to Love
12. The Star of Love
13. Music is the Soul of Love
14. Love in the East
15. Theirs to Eternity
16. A Paradise on Earth
17. Love Wins in Berlin
18. In Search of Love
19. Love Rescues Rosanna
20. A Heart in Heaven
21. The House of Happiness
22. Royalty Defeated by Love
23. The White Witch
24. They Sought Love
25. Love is the Reason for Living
26. They Found Their Way to Heaven
27. Learning to Love
28. Journey to Happiness
29. A Kiss in the Desert
30. The Heart of Love
31. The Richness of Love
32. For Ever and Ever

FOR EVER AND EVER

BARBARA CARTLAND

Barbaracartland.com Ltd

Copyright © 2007 by Cartland Promotions
First published on the internet in May
2007 by Barbaracartland.com

ISBN 978-1-905155-41-5

The characters and situations in this book are entirely imaginary and bear no relation to any real person or actual happening.

This book is sold subject to the condition that it shall not, by way of trade or otherwise, be lent, resold, hired out or otherwise circulated without the publisher's prior consent.

No part of this publication may be reproduced or transmitted in any form or by any means, electronically or mechanically, including photocopying, recording or any information storage or retrieval, without the prior permission in writing from the publisher.

Printed and bound in Great Britain by CLE Print Ltd. of St Ives, Cambridgeshire.

THE BARBARA CARTLAND PINK COLLECTION

Barbara Cartland was the most prolific bestselling author in the history of the world. She was frequently in the Guinness Book of Records for writing more books in a year than any other living author. In fact her most amazing literary feat was when her publishers asked for more Barbara Cartland romances, she doubled her output from 10 books a year to over 20 books a year, when she was 77.

She went on writing continuously at this rate for 20 years and wrote her last book at the age of 97, thus completing 400 books between the ages of 77 and 97.

Her publishers finally could not keep up with this phenomenal output, so at her death she left 160 unpublished manuscripts, something again that no other author has ever achieved.

Now the exciting news is that these 160 original unpublished Barbara Cartland books are already being published and by Barbaracartland.com exclusively on the internet, as the international web is the best possible way of reaching so many Barbara Cartland readers around the world.

The 160 books are published monthly and will be numbered in sequence.

The series is called the Pink Collection as a tribute to Barbara Cartland whose favourite colour was pink and it became very much her trademark over the years.

The Barbara Cartland Pink Collection is published only on the internet. Log on to www.barbaracartland.com to find out how you can purchase the books monthly as they are published, and take out a subscription that will ensure that all subsequent editions are delivered to you by mail order to your home.

NEW

Barbaracartland.com is proud to announce the publication of ten new Audio Books for the first time as CDs. They are favourite Barbara Cartland stories read by well-known actors and actresses and each story extends to 4 or 5 CDs. The Audio Books are as follows :

The Patient Bridegroom	The Passion and the Flower
A Challenge of Hearts	Little White Doves of Love
A Train to Love	The Prince and the Pekinese
The Unbroken Dream	A King in Love
The Cruel Count	A Sign of Love

More Audio Books will be published in the future and the above titles can be purchased by logging on to the website www.barbaracartland.com or please write to the address below.

If you do not have access to a computer, you can write for information about the Barbara Cartland Pink Collection and the Barbara Cartland Audio Books to the following address :

Barbara Cartland.com Ltd.
Camfield Place,
Hatfield,
Hertfordshire AL9 6JE
United Kingdom.
Telephone: +44 (0)1707 642629
Fax: +44 (0)1707 663041

THE LATE DAME BARBARA CARTLAND

Barbara Cartland who sadly died in May 2000 at the age of nearly 99 was the world's most famous romantic novelist who wrote 723 books in her lifetime with worldwide sales of over 1 billion copies and her books were translated into 36 different languages.

As well as romantic novels, she wrote historical biographies, 6 autobiographies, theatrical plays, books of advice on life, love, vitamins and cookery. She also found time to be a political speaker and television and radio personality.

She wrote her first book at the age of 21 and this was called *Jigsaw*. It became an immediate bestseller and sold 100,000 copies in hardback and was translated into 6 different languages. She wrote continuously throughout her life, writing bestsellers for an astonishing 76 years. Her books have always been immensely popular in the United States, where in 1976 her current books were at numbers 1 & 2 in the B. Dalton bestsellers list, a feat never achieved before or since by any author.

Barbara Cartland became a legend in her own lifetime and will be best remembered for her wonderful romantic novels, so loved by her millions of readers throughout the world.

Her books will always be treasured for their moral message, her pure and innocent heroines, her good looking and dashing heroes and above all her belief that the power of love is more important than anything else in everyone's life.

"All the greatest music, literature and music ever written is always about love."

Barbara Cartland

CHAPTER ONE
1895

"Goodbye, Mama! Goodbye, Papa!"

Viola wept profusely as she threw two handfuls of earth into the open grave that had been freshly dug that morning. As she let the earth fall, she felt so utterly alone that it was as if the other mourners, who stood around her, were not present.

Viola Brookfield had only just celebrated her twenty-first birthday when it happened – the tragic series of events that led to both her parents being killed.

They had set off, one bright Spring morning, in their new automobile for a second honeymoon in the South of France.

Viola had not wanted to be left alone in the big house in Connaught Square that was only moments away from Hyde Park.

"Please do not go. I shall be so lonely," she had implored them as Morton, the butler, supervised the loading of trunks onto the new motor car.

"Darling, we shall not be long – it is only a week and then we shall return with lots of presents for you," her mother had said, kissing her daughter.

"Mama, I do not care for presents, I would prefer that

we were together, as a family."

"We shall be one once more upon our return," answered her father, whose dashing good looks still made the ladies' heads turn.

Reluctantly Viola had waved them off as the automobile sprang noisily into life and slowly inched away from the kerb.

Her last sight of them was as they turned the corner into Connaught Street, her mother waving furiously with the long scarf that secured her hat wound around her elegant throat and its ends floating in the breeze like bunting at a fair. Her lovely face was alive with pleasure and expectation, while her husband concentrated on the task in hand – looking straight ahead, his face was set into an expression of grim concentration.

He had not looked back.

Viola could not stop berating herself for not being more insistent that they remain in London. For that was the last time she saw either of them.

The headlamps on the car were not strong enough to light their way through the dark French night and, just outside of Nice, the automobile spun off a sharp bend and down a cliff taking them to their deaths.

She remembered the day that the Policeman had come to the door, asking to see her. Morton's grave face alerted her that something terrible had happened.

"There is an Officer of the Law to see you, Miss Viola," he had said, his voice shaking as he wrung his hands.

Viola had felt as if she was about to faint, but composed herself sufficiently to walk to the morning room. The Policeman had not sat down and was standing by the door, ready to make a hasty exit as soon as he had imparted his news.

"Miss Brookfield?" he had asked, as she entered the

room. "I am afraid that I have some bad news for you. It is your mother and father."

Viola had been forced to sit down, as her legs began to turn to jelly. She barely heard the remainder of what he said, as she was only conscious of a searing pain that gripped her heart and squeezed it until she could scarcely breathe.

The Policeman had left and she remained sitting in her chair for an age afterwards. Hot tears scalded her cheeks as she moaned softly to herself.

Morton had not known what to do with her when he entered the room some time later and so called for Milly, Viola's lady's maid.

Milly rushed to Viola's side and helped her upstairs to her bedroom, where she remained for the rest of the day, weeping endlessly, refusing food or drink.

A pall of silence fell upon the house and so it remained, with the windows masked with heavy curtains like closed eyelids, until the day of the funeral.

And now just three weeks later the Brookfields were finally being laid to rest in All Souls cemetery in Kensal Green.

As the crowd around the grave began to depart, Viola could not tear herself away.

"Just a moment longer," she said to her Cousin Agnes, who came up and softly took her arm, "I do not think that I can bear to say the final farewell and leave."

"Shall I ask for your carriage to be brought to the end of the avenue?" asked Agnes.

"Please, a little longer," pleaded Viola.

Agnes moved away from her grieving cousin and joined the throng who were making their way back to their own transport.

Viola had not wanted to replace her parents' wrecked

car and now, superstitiously, she refused to travel in any conveyance that did not have a horse pulling it.

A chilly wind suddenly blew across the cemetery and Viola shivered. Her black satin cape was thin and did not provide adequate protection.

"Come, miss, the carriage is here," suggested Milly, gently.

She and the other servants had stood respectfully at the back of the crowd around the grave and were now making their way to Kensal Road to catch the tram.

"I will come with you, miss, if that is what you want," offered the girl.

Viola tore her eyes away from the deep trench. She could no longer bear to look at the expensive coffins, placed one on top of the other, with their ornate brass handles and sober plaques.

"Goodbye, Mama. Goodbye, Papa," she repeated softly feeling as if she was leaving a part of herself down in that muddy trench with them.

Dabbing her eyes, Viola followed Milly to the waiting phaeton. The horses were a pair of black stallions, especially selected for the sombre occasion and the windows were swathed in black curtains.

Stepping inside, Viola was glad that they could be pulled to and obscure her from prying eyes.

*

The past few weeks had passed slowly. Each day she had roamed about the house, weeping quietly to herself as she recalled happier times.

Every corner held a memory for her and so, when the letter from her aunt in India arrived five days after the funeral, she found herself not adverse to her proposal.

"*Dearest Niece*," it read.

"I can scarcely bring myself to believe the terrible events that have taken place since I last wrote to you. To think that only a month ago, I was writing to congratulate you upon the occasion of your twenty-first birthday and now I find my hand shaking with grief as I write this letter.

Lord Wakefield, your uncle, and myself, your loving aunt, cannot find the words to describe our desolation. To think that I might never look upon my dear sister's face again fills me with the utmost misery.

Your uncle and I have had long discussions about what will now happen to you, and we think it best if you came to live with us in Mandavi for the foreseeable future.

You need to be around your family at this sad time and I would not hear of you going anywhere else. Perhaps, by being together we can lessen our grief.

I realise that the journey will be long and arduous, but if you feel you would like to accept our offer, please write at once and we shall make arrangements for you to be met at Bombay and accompanied on the journey North to Mandavi.

Fondest love,

Your Aunt Mary."

'India,' sighed Viola. The very name conjured up a continent of untold exoticism and mystery.

Lady Wakefield was her mother's elder sister and, from what her mother had told her, it had been a whirlwind romance and wedding. Lord Wakefield was a very important man in the Province where they lived and was the Governor.

Although there was a Prince Potentate, it was Lord Wakefield who reported directly to Her Majesty's Viceroy.

Viola had not seen Lord Wakefield for many years. Although Aunt Mary had visited a few years earlier when the couple had been summoned to Court, Uncle Hugo had not accompanied her to their house in Connaught Square.

'I wonder if he looks very old now?' she asked herself. 'He must be at least fifty, as he was a lot older than Aunt Mary and Mama.'

She remembered Uncle Hugo as being a stern man with a clipped moustache and an erect posture. However, he had always been kind to her and usually brought her small presents – as a child, her nursery was full of carved wooden elephants lavishly decorated with red silken tassels that smelled of spices and strange perfumes.

Viola arose from her seat and folded the letter carefully. She did not need to think over her aunt's offer for very long. She had already decided that she could not stay on in Connaught Square.

'It will mean having to shut up the house,' she thought to herself, as she walked towards her father's old study, 'and there is the problem of our house on the Isle of Wight.'

Viola's mother had inherited the large sprawling manor house from a maiden aunt, when Aunt Mary had refused it after the old lady had died.

It had always been a place of rest and retreat. It boasted one of the finest stables in the South of England and even Queen Victoria herself had been known to borrow mounts from its vast stock of superior beasts.

'*The horses*,' thought Viola, suddenly overwhelmed at the responsibility that had fallen upon her young shoulders. 'What will I do with them if I go to India?'

She thought of Jet and Sable, Flash and Thunder – each had their own personality and Viola had mastered riding them all – even the feisty Copper, whom her father had struggled to tame.

Viola wandered over to the study window and looked out over the Square. Pulling back the heavy curtain, she could see that life was going on as normal – the chimney sweep was crossing the road with his band of boys, the dairyman was calling with his deliveries – yet, inside number 30, it was as if time was standing still.

'Mama and Papa would not want me to moulder away here when I am still young and attractive,' she pondered. 'How many times did Papa take me to one side and tell me that I should enjoy myself now before I married?'

Marriage! It was the last thing on Viola's mind. She had only experience of a few mild flirtations that had come to nothing – the charming Captain of the Queen's Guards whom she had met last summer and there had been Georgie Carolan, the son of an Irish Peer who had charmed her with his lilting accent and fine manners.

'No, the idea of marriage will be quite out of the question for the next year or so. Even if some of my friends are finding husbands, I declare that, at the moment, I would not care if I was to be an old maid for life!'

Just then Milly came in to the study, holding a white linen dress.

"Beggin' your pardon, miss, but I wondered what you wished me to do with this? I was goin' through your wardrobe and it was at the bottom."

Viola held the soft fabric with a hint of regret. She would not be wearing white this summer, as she would be in strict mourning for at least a year.

"Please have it dyed black, Milly – I shall need it where I am going."

Milly gave her a curious look.

"And where is that, miss?"

"India," breathed Viola. "I have made a decision. My aunt has written and invited me to stay with her indefinitely."

Milly frowned as she took back the dress. Viola could see that the prospect did not excite her for, as her lady's maid, she would be expected to travel with her.

"You do not seem too pleased at the idea," remarked Viola.

The girl flushed bright red and then stammered,

"Oh, miss, I couldn't go to India – not with my mother in such poor health. It would kill her sure as eggs is eggs, miss, if I were to go high-tailin' it off to India."

Viola paused and reflected for a moment.

"I will not force you to come with me, Milly. If you do not wish to go, I shall make enquiries amongst my friends to see if we can find you another post. I intend to shut up the house and only Morton and Mrs. Gilks will be kept on."

"I wish you were stayin', miss," said Milly, with her eyes filling, "you've been so good me."

"And I will continue to be so," replied Viola. "I promise that I will make sure you have a place to go to, now – will you ask Morton and Mrs. Gilks to come upstairs? I wish to inform them of my intentions."

Milly bundled the gown under her arm and bobbed a curtsy, leaving Viola to reflect upon her decision.

"I have always wanted to see India," she said out loud, "and now, I shall!"

*

Morton and Mrs. Gilks took the news well that Viola intended to shut up the house.

"Mrs. Gilks, you will accompany me to the house at Cowes to help me select who to keep on there, if you will," added Viola, after she had told them of her plans.

"I would be glad to do so, miss," replied the housekeeper.

"And Morton, if and when I intend to return, I shall write and inform you so that you may begin to hire new staff. In the meantime, I shall expect both you and Mrs. Gilks to remain here after my departure and see that the house is maintained."

Viola was amazed at how coolly she was dealing with everything. It was not so long ago that she did not have a care in the world, but the accident had changed everything.

As soon as she had dismissed Morton and Mrs. Gilks, she sat down to write to her aunt, telling her that she would be delighted to come out to India and would she please make the arrangements for her travel from Bombay to Mandavi.

'There, it is done,' she muttered, as she addressed the letter with a flourish.

*

The next few weeks flew by in a flurry of activity. Viola had many calls to pay to friends and what family remained in London. Cousin Agnes was beside herself that she was leaving.

"My brother, Albie, has a friend who is serving out in Mandavi – he is the Earl of Devonport – you must pay him a visit whilst you are there. I shall make Albie write you a letter of introduction."

Viola coloured deeply – she did not fancy the idea of visiting a strange gentleman in the least.

"Oh, do not worry. As he is staying with some friends of ours it will be quite correct for you to visit," said Agnes, realising that what she said had sounded a little off colour. "I simply meant that it would be nice if you were not without new friends in India. I have heard it can be a lonely place."

"Thank you, Agnes, it is so kind of you to think of me in that way," replied Viola, with a sigh of relief. "I shall miss you all very much and I shall be glad of a friendly face. Why is he out there?"

"Oh, some government business. Albie will never tell me what it is. Frightfully top secret, apparently. But I do know that Albie is awfully fond of him and says that he's a good sort."

Viola already liked the sound of this man with an air of mystery.

As she left to return to Connaught Square, Agnes embraced her warmly.

"Promise me that you will write often," she said, her voice quivering with emotion. "I shall miss you."

As her carriage sped along by the Serpentine, Viola allowed herself one last lingering look.

'In a few days, I shall be on my way to a new life and all this will become a memory.'

She opened her bag and looked once again at the piece of paper with the Earl of Devonport's address in Mandavi written on it.

'I wonder what he will be like,' she mused, 'I do hope that he is kind and good company.'

*

All too soon, the day dawned when she would begin her long journey to India.

Morton had made enquiries for her and had booked her a good cabin on a steamship that was bound to Bombay from Southampton.

Viola was delighted, because that meant that she would be able to visit the house at Cowes one last time before she departed.

As had been arranged, Mrs. Gilks accompanied her on the train to Portsmouth and from there, they took the ferry across the Solent to Ryde.

The Brookfield family phaeton was waiting for them at the entrance to the pier.

Viola felt quite tearful as she clambered on board and sank back into the familiar comfortable surroundings.

An hour later, she alighted outside the Manor house at East Cowes. The views across the Solent always filled her with comfort, but today, she felt an overwhelming sense of sadness.

Mrs. Gilks went on into the house while Viola made her way to the stables. She was looking forward to seeing Jet, Copper and all the others.

Bartholomew, the head groom, looked up from his set of curry combs as Viola walked into the stable yard.

"Miss Viola," he cried, putting them down. "Come here, lass – we are all so sorry about your mother and father."

The groom did not have any truck with ceremony or what was considered correct. He simply walked up to Viola and put his big hand on her shoulder.

"They were good folk," he continued, "and we miss them so much already."

"Thank you," whispered Viola, her voice hoarse with emotion, "I miss them very much, too. I am afraid that I will not have time to take Copper out as I am only here overnight. My ship leaves on tomorrow's evening tide."

"They be saying that you're bound for India."

"That is true, Bartholomew, and I am expecting that you and the stable boys will tend to the horses as you would your own children."

She left him to his work and wandered over to the stable block. How she loved the smell of straw and leather.

'I do hope that I will be able to go riding when I am in India,' she thought. 'I am certain that Mama used to say how much Aunt Mary enjoyed going out on horseback, so perhaps I will not have to miss my horses too much.'

Copper was in his stall, pulling contentedly on a bale of straw.

Viola called to him softly and the big chestnut stallion

snorted and ambled over to the door. She stroked his muscular neck and inhaled his scent.

"I am sorry I cannot take you out today, boy," she whispered. "It may be some time before we see each other again, but you make sure you do not torment the others, you hear?"

The horse snorted and nodded his head as if he had understood every word. Viola hated to leave him, more than any of the others.

She turned and walked back across the yard to the house. Slipping in through the kitchen door, she startled Mrs. Gilks who was in deep conversation with Mrs. Miller, the housekeeper at the Manor.

They bobbed curtsies as she swept past on her way to the drawing room. Inside, the clock ticked softly and it was as peaceful as ever.

In fact it looked just as the family had left it at Christmas.

Viola stood by the fireplace and looked into the empty grate – she recalled how her mother had sung and played the piano, whilst her father had accompanied her in a fine bass.

Tears filled her brown eyes and she stared at her reflection in the mahogany mirror that hung above the mantelpiece.

Even in tears, Viola still looked beautiful. Her thick blonde hair was swept up into a loose chignon and thin tendrils had escaped to frame her lovely face.

Viola stared hard into her own eyes and her heartbreak was plain to see.

Suddenly, she was startled by a low cough behind her. She spun round to see Mrs. Gilks with a sheaf of papers in her hand.

"I'm sorry to disturb you, miss, but your passport and

travelling papers have just arrived."

"So, I am really on my way," she said in a low voice as she looked at her passport. The photograph in it was her, yet she did not recognise herself. It had been taken the year that her parents had taken her to the South of France for a holiday.

Now, she was bound for the East and to a country she knew very little about. She had no idea which language was spoken, or what the customs might be.

"Thank you, Mrs. Gilks. I will take dinner in my room tonight as we have much to do tomorrow before my ship sails from Southampton."

The housekeeper left the room and Viola sat down at the piano. Absent-mindedly running her fingers over the keys, she decided to go to the library and find an atlas, so that she could plot her journey.

In the library Viola clambered up a set of wooden steps to where she knew the maps of Asia were kept. Taking down one of the red leather-bound volumes, she blew off the dust and carried it down to the table. The pages were yellow with age, but the maps were still clear and bright.

Viola ran her finger along from Bombay up the coast to the Gulf of Kutch.

'Mandavi, Mandavi,' she repeated to herself.

Eventually, she found it.

'It seems a long way from Bombay, so I suppose we shall go there by train.'

She had heard her uncle telling stories of the railways in India and how even pigs and goats were crammed into the carriages with the human occupants. Viola wondered if that kind of thing happened in first class and shuddered. She did not fancy the idea of sitting next to a goat on the long trip to Mandavi!

Closing the book, she suddenly felt overwhelmed. She missed her mother and father more than ever and everything she did seemed so difficult. She had gone from being carefree to assuming so much responsibility and did not know which way to turn.

'I wish Mama and Papa were here,' she intoned for the hundredth time that day. 'I wish I did not think that it is all a bad dream and that they will suddenly turn up at the door alive and well.'

Viola felt incredibly nervous at the prospect of a long sea journey on her own, and Milly had made it plain that she would not be travelling with her. The girl had now gone to work for Cousin Agnes.

It had been the ideal solution but, even so, Viola missed her little maid with her funny ways and nimble fingers. When she had left, she had presented Viola with a filet-crocheted set of handkerchiefs – "for the journey", she had said.

Wandering out of the library, Viola saw the stack of trunks piled up in the Hall. The leather tags all read, "*Miss Viola Brookfield, Mandavi via Bombay, India.*"

'I still cannot believe that I am leaving tomorrow.'

She ran her hands over the smooth leather trunks. She was taking the noon ferry to Portsmouth and the ship to India was due to sail at five o'clock.

The journey East would take several weeks.

'I just wish that I was not so frightened,' thought Viola, as she turned to walk upstairs to her room, 'but I am determined not to change my mind.'

*

Viola dined alone in her room that evening and retired to bed early. The next morning, she was up before the maid had brought her tea tray and then she took one last turn around the grounds after breakfast.

After an early luncheon, Viola gathered her things together and made ready to leave. She could not prevent the tears from running down her face as she bade farewell to Mrs. Gilks.

"Please take good care of yourself, miss," said the housekeeper, fondly, "I am sure that the Master and Mistress are up in Heaven looking down on you. They'll make sure you come to no harm."

Viola was too choked to respond. Mrs Gilks had served the Brookfields since before she was born.

'She is almost like family to me,' thought Viola, as she waited for the carriage to be brought to the front of the Manor.

She tried not to look back as she left, but it was impossible.

'My old life is at an end,' she murmured with tears in her eyes.

Much later at Southampton, Viola looked up at the massive steamship that was to take her to India. All around her, there were so many people yet she felt so alone.

She boarded the ship and was taken to her cabin.

Viola did not go up on deck as the ship pulled away from the dock. She did not want to see the passengers waving to loved ones who stood on the quayside furiously waving back.

After a while, she heard the engines roar to life beneath her feet as she sat quietly on her bed.

'Goodbye England, I wonder when I will see you again,' she mumbled, as the ship churned a deep furrow through the sea on its way out of Southampton docks.

CHAPTER TWO

The journey to India was every bit as long as Viola had anticipated.

For the first few days, she was terribly seasick and was confined to her cabin.

And then, she began to enjoy her daily strolls on deck – even though she frequently had to fend off the unwanted attentions of various young gentlemen.

A kindly dowager, who was travelling with a young female companion, took her under her wing and so she spent much of her time talking to her and playing whist.

Along the way, they stopped off at many interesting ports and Viola was enthralled by all the sights.

When her new friends left the ship at Bombay to catch the train to Delhi, Viola wept almost as much as when she had left England.

Stepping off the ship on to Indian soil, Viola's senses were assaulted by the strange and wonderful sights and smells of India.

Although she had gradually become accustomed to the increasing heat, she felt as if she had walked into a steamy kitchen as she ambled along the quayside to the Shipping Office where she had arranged to meet Aunt Mary's chaperone.

'If I did not know for certain that I was awake, I would

swear I was having a vivid dream,' mused Viola, as she pushed past an ox which wandered around with no driver and small children who ran hither and thither in very few clothes.

At the Shipping Office, the travelling companion who had been sent to escort her was sitting on a wooden bench, awaiting her arrival.

He was a small, neat man with the air of someone who had spent time in the Army.

"Miss Brookfield?" he asked in a soft Scottish accent. "I am George MacDonald. Your uncle has sent me to accompany you to Mandavi. I trust you have had a good journey?"

Viola passed her hand over her brow – the office was rather stuffy and she felt extremely hot in her black silk dress.

"Most interesting, thank you. Although I confess that I am glad to be on solid ground again."

"I have arranged for your luggage to be sent on ahead," said Mr. MacDonald, "your aunt will have told you what to expect, I trust?"

"She did, but nothing has prepared me for this!"

George MacDonald chuckled to himself and then nodded sagely.

"Yes, most think that when they first arrive in India. It is just so different."

Just then, a young Indian boy ran in and said something to him that Viola did not understand. She was impressed when he replied in the boy's tongue.

"Which language is that you were speaking?"

"Hindi, but there are many different dialects spoken on the Subcontinent. In Mandavi, they speak Kutchi and Gujarati."

"Are they difficult to pick up?"

Mr. MacDonald gave another gentle laugh.

"You will find the languages here utterly different from anything you will have ever heard," he said, "but come, we must get to the station for the next part of our journey, as there is just one train a day that goes directly to Mandavi."

He ushered Viola out to a waiting carriage and she was relieved that the motor car had not yet reached India.

The steam train was belching smoke as they climbed into a first class carriage.

Viola had found it incredible that both people and animals were crammed into the other carriages and that there were even people hanging onto the roof!

Viola sighed. She was so tired and yet, they still had so far to travel. Her journey was beginning to feel like one of those horrid dreams that never end.

*

They arrived in Mandavi three days later feeling tired, thirsty and dusty.

Viola's hair was dirty and smelly from the coal dust that blew in through the windows and she had not been able to have a bath since she had arrived in Bombay. How she longed for soap and clean sheets!

She waited on the platform while Mr. MacDonald chatted in Kutchi to the Station Master. He returned to where she was standing with a broad grin on his face.

"Mr. Methi says that your luggage arrived yesterday and has already been delivered to the house," he beamed. "Most unusual for India."

"Thank Heavens. I was concerned that it would end up in Delhi!"

"Come, Lord Wakefield has sent a carriage for us and it is outside," he gestured towards the exit and soon Viola found herself in a crush of people who were all pushing to get out of the narrow picket gate.

A liveried Indian stood patiently by the splendid carriage. It was a little old-fashioned, Viola thought, but then again, Lord and Lady Wakefield had been in India for nearly twenty-three years.

"Welcome to Mandavi, *memsahib*," said the Indian, bowing low. He was no more than a boy – nineteen at most, thought Viola, with a fine profile and warm brown eyes.

"How far is the house?" asked Viola, as Mr. MacDonald joined her inside the open carriage.

"We shall be there in about ten minutes," he replied.

After a short ride, the carriage passed through ornate gates and along a drive lined with trees that hung heavy with fruit that Viola had never seen before.

The house was long and low with only one story and Viola could see that a pleasant veranda ran around it and that the gardens were full of huge exotic blooms.

"Viola. Viola."

It was Aunt Mary. Viola jumped down from the carriage as her aunt came running towards her.

"Darling. I cannot believe that you are here."

Her aunt was weeping with joy and held Viola so tightly that she could hardly breathe. Aunt Mary let her go and took a good long look at her niece.

"You are the very image of your mother when she was your age," she exclaimed, wiping a tear from her eye. "Your poor, dear mother."

All of a sudden, Viola became aware of the figure of a tall man standing some distance away from her aunt. She looked up and discovered that it was her uncle, looking stiff and awkward as if he did not wish to be present.

Viola gasped – he was not the same man she had last

seen when she was twelve years old. Where was the friendly uncle who had indulged her with presents and called her his favourite?

"Uncle Hugo?" she said, querulously, afraid to embrace him.

"Welcome to our house," he said rather quietly.

"Hugo, is that all you have to say to her? She has come halfway round the world to see us. You must not take any notice of him, he is terribly preoccupied with this Russian nonsense," said her aunt, linking her arm through Viola's.

"What Russian nonsense?" asked Viola, a little fearfully.

"Oh, it is nothing to worry yourself about. We occasionally have a little trouble with the Russians attempting to storm the frontiers of Afghanistan. They are over a thousand miles away, so it is really nothing to be concerned about."

"I did not realise that Russia was so close."

"Oh, they have to go through both Turkistan and Afghanistan before they can reach India. It really is just a little trouble, I promise you."

Even so, Viola was concerned. She had heard mutterings on the ship about *the Great Game* to do with India and Russia, but she had not really understood what it was all about and so had not paid attention when discussion had turned to the subject.

'I shall ask Uncle Hugo about it once I have settled in,' she thought, as they walked into the house.

Viola noticed that her uncle stood at the entrance to the hallway – a strange look upon his face.

"So like her mother," she heard him murmur as she passed by. His voice was so low that she had barely caught his words.

Viola flushed a deep red and hid her face. There was something about her uncle's manner that made her feel distinctly uncomfortable.

"Dear, do come into the drawing room, it is much cooler at this time of day."

Her aunt's voice broke into her thoughts as she tried to hide her discomfort.

"Coming, aunt," she called, walking quickly towards the drawing room.

"Lime juice and water – they call it *nimbu pani* out here," said her aunt, offering her a glass of pale liquid. "Do not worry, it does not taste tart – Anjali, our cook, put plenty of *jaggeree* in it."

"*Jaggeree?*" asked Viola.

"It is a kind of sugar, darling."

Viola sipped at the drink and found it simply delicious. Her dry throat was crying out for liquid and it slipped down beautifully.

"Now, sit down and tell me all your news."

Viola found a comfortable chair and sank down gratefully. She could not wait to ask if she could take a bath.

"There is not much to tell – " she began.

"But the funeral. I am so sorry I could not be there. I cry every day thinking of your dear Mama. Hugo has been beside himself with grief as well. He was so fond of her – " her voice trailed off as Viola caught a pained look in her eyes that she could not explain.

"However, if we have been upset, I cannot imagine how distraught you must be. Losing both your parents and at such a young age."

"It has been very difficult," replied Viola, finishing her drink, "there has been so much to do – the houses, the servants – "

"Will you sell them?"

"No, I have let most of the servants go and kept on the butlers and housekeepers. And, of course, there are the stables at the house on the Isle of Wight. I could not bear to part with the horses so I have retained the stable staff."

"You will find that there are some fine horses locally that you may ride on our estate," said Aunt Mary, replenishing Viola's glass. "You must ask your uncle to take you riding one afternoon – that is, if he can find the time. He is presently so busy."

"To do with the Russians?" asked Viola.

Her aunt hesitated before replying and then simply nodded her head.

"Ah, look," she cried, grateful for the interruption, "here is Mirupa. She will take you to your room and look after you. We will have dinner at seven o'clock."

The girl was as slender as a reed and beautiful. She put her delicate hands together and bowed her head to Viola.

"*Namaste,* Miss Brookfield, welcome."

Viola was not certain how she should respond, so she simply smiled.

Mirupa smiled back and gracefully indicated that Viola should follow her.

Viola took an instant liking to Mirupa. She seemed to glide along the floor as she turned to go upstairs. Viola could not help but stare at the girl's clothing that seemed to consist of acres of fabric, wound around her slender frame, and the shiny plait of black hair that hung down her back. It was so long, she could have sat on it.

Mirupa opened the door to a light airy room with wooden blinds at the windows. Viola looked with curiosity at the netting over the bed and touched it.

"That is a mosquito net," Mirupa informed her, "you

sleep under it at night."

Viola nodded. She had heard about malaria and had packed a bottle of quinine just in case.

"Tell me, Mirupa, what do you call the dress you are wearing?"

Mirupa smiled to herself as if she had heard the same question a thousand times from English ladies.

"It is called a *saree*."

"It is beautiful," exclaimed Viola, "and so intricate."

"If *memsahib* would like me to show her how to wear one, I shall bring one."

Viola clapped her hands together in delight,

"That would be wonderful, but tell me, you speak perfect English – I confess that I did not expect Aunt Mary's – servants to be so – "

She stumbled over her words and suddenly felt embarrassed at her naivety.

Mirupa smiled again, and replied,

"You did not expect me to be educated? In India, I come from a good family and my parents pride themselves on being modern, so I was taught the same subjects as my brothers. We all speak English as well as our own language."

"I am glad to hear that. I too, was fortunate that my parents insisted I apply myself to my studies. Sadly, they are no longer with us as they died recently."

"Oh, *memsahib*! I am so sorry," cried Mirupa, pity welling up in her huge brown eyes, "and that is why you are here in India?"

"Yes," answered Viola, taking from her bag the treasured photograph that she had brought with her. "Look, these are my parents."

"So noble. Now, if you will excuse me, *memsahib*, I

shall fill your bath for you. It is in the dressing room."

Viola could have cried with joy, as she had never felt so dirty and sticky.

"Thank you. Thank you. Until it is ready, I will go and have a look around. Is my aunt still in the drawing room?"

"Yes, *memsahib*."

"Then I shall return shortly."

Viola kicked off her shoes and wandered barefoot out into the landing.

'There are so many things that are different about India,' she thought. 'Servants being able to converse in another language. I cannot imagine poor Milly managing even one word of French.'

The landing was painted white and hung with fabulous works of art that Aunt Mary had brought from England. Viola looked at a portrait of an elegant Georgian lady and wondered if she might be a relative.

'I must ask Aunt Mary who she is,' she resolved, 'there is so much that I do not know about our family and now that Mama is gone, she is the only one I can ask.'

As she walked downstairs, she noticed that her aunt was talking to a servant about the dinner menu. The old lady looked as if she was too ancient to walk around the veranda, let alone make a meal, but as Viola was discovering, India was full of surprises.

"Ah, Viola, dearest. Anjali is going to make us a feast to celebrate your arrival – I do hope that you will enjoy it. Is there anything you do not eat?"

"I am so famished I declare that I could eat whatever is put in front of me."

"Then, Anjali will cook her famous chicken dish – it is

typical of the area and not too spicy. I think you will enjoy it."

Viola was a little unsure whether she would enjoy Indian food but she did not say anything. She had heard that it was a spicy and fiery concoction of strange ingredients. One of her father's aunts had lived in India for a while and had complained bitterly that she could not stomach the food.

"Aunt, I have something to ask you," began Viola.

"What is it, child? You must speak frankly – we are your family now."

"Why could you not have come to mother and father's funeral? I had expected you to be there."

"I am so very sorry, darling, but I could not leave India. Your Uncle Hugo has been so very busy with this Russian business – "

Her voice trailed off and she looked downwards, almost as if she had something to hide. Viola was beginning to think that the situation was perhaps more serious than her aunt had at first led her to believe.

"Aunt, are we in danger?"

"Not at all. We are perfectly safe and I am just a perfect fool to worry over trifles. Tell me, is your room comfortable and do you have everything you need? I hope it meets with your approval."

Viola noticed that Aunt Mary had skilfully moved the conversation away from the difficult topic.

"It is lovely, thank you, and Mirupa is so nice. She is now filling a bath."

"We dine at seven, so you have plenty of time to refresh yourself. You will soon become accustomed to our way of life here. I have made arrangements for you to meet people, so that you will not be lonely. There will be times, you see, that I shall have to leave you to your own devices."

"I am used to amusing myself," replied Viola. "I am, after all, an only child."

"Of course, you were not fortunate enough to have a brother or sister."

"Mama had a terrible time when I was born and the doctors told her that she could have no more children. I never used to mind as I rather liked having my parents all to myself, but now, I wish I had a brother or sister to share my burdens."

"It isn't always easy to have a more beautiful younger sister," commented her aunt in a rather strange tone of voice. She looked pensively out of the window and Viola suddenly felt rather awkward. What could her aunt be referring to?

The tension was broken when one of her aunt's servants entered the room.

"Ah, Dinesh, this is my niece, Miss Viola. She will be staying with us for as long as she wishes. Viola, Dinesh is our butler – he used to be your uncle's batman the Army."

Viola thought him an extremely handsome man for his age. His hair was still as black as jet and his eyes were an unusual shade of light brown. She noticed a large scar over his eyebrow and wondered how it had got there.

The scar reminded her of Albie, her cousin, who sported a similar mark and it made her think of his friend whom Agnes had been so keen for her to meet.

Surely, her aunt would know him?

"Aunt, have you, by any chance, made the acquaintance of Lord Devonport?"

"Why, yes, I have. Such a charming young man – he often dines with us."

"Cousin Agnes was keen for me to meet him as he is a friend of her brother."

"Ah," nodded Aunt Mary, "that would be because he

has the finest stable this side of Bombay. Clever Agnes. She knew that you would be missing your horses."

"You are so right. I miss Copper, Thunder and Jet so much already. I had hoped that I would be able to explore the area on horseback, but did not know who would be able to accompany me. I hope that this gentleman will agree to do so."

"I am certain that he will. Shall I invite him over for tea tomorrow? And so you can meet him and ask him yourself."

Viola suddenly felt a little shy, as Mirupa appeared in the doorway.

"Your bath is ready, *memsahib*," she said quietly.

"Now you must go, dearest," said Aunt Mary. "I hope that you have brought some lighter clothing with you?"

Viola looked down at her fussy silk dress in dismay.

"I have only one linen dress that my maid dyed black. I confess that I did not realise how hot it would be."

"Then we shall have to go into town and have some new gowns made for you. The cotton out here is particularly fine and light, although the natives think us strange for wearing black when someone has died. They wear white, you see."

"Really?"

"Now, dear, run along and have your bath."

Viola followed Mirupa upstairs. She could not wait to bathe and change.

She sank into the refreshing water gratefully to find that Mirupa had scented the water with a strange but wonderful oil that clung to her skin.

Viola reflected upon her journey and how she now felt so far away from England and all its terrible memories.

'I almost feel as if Mama and Papa had never existed,'

she mused, quite shocked at herself at such a thought, 'yet the pain is with me constantly.'

She wondered if it would be really dreadful if she did not wear mourning out here in India. After all, had not Aunt Mary said that the locals wore white when bereaved? That sounded infinitely much more sensible and more practical.

'I wonder if Mama and Papa would be upset if I did not wear black?'

But there was no reply forthcoming and Viola wept into her bath water.

"Oh, this will not help me at all," she sniffed, as Mirupa hurried towards her with a large towel.

"Is *memsahib* feeling unwell?" she asked, kindly.

"No, I am quite well, thank you. I was thinking of my Mama and Papa and it made me feel sad."

Mirupa nodded as if she understood.

'Everyone has been so very kind,' murmured Viola to her own reflection in the dressing table mirror.

She looked on the dressing table for her brushes, but they had not been put out with the rest of her toilet set.

'Mirupa must have been unable to find them or maybe she has put them away by mistake.'

Viola looked around the room and searched in the wardrobe, the chest of drawers and the drawers of the marble washstand, but the brushes were not there.

Finally her eyes happened upon a built-in cupboard to the left of her bed.

'Perhaps she put them in that cupboard,' she wondered, stretching her hand out to pull at the metal handle.

But the cupboard door appeared to be stuck. Viola pulled and pulled and it was only after she tugged so hard that it made her fingers red, that it finally opened.

Peering inside, Viola could see that there was nothing

of hers. It had obviously not been opened for a long time as it smelt musty.

And then she saw what appeared to be a photo frame with its glass and contents placed face down.

Even though she knew she should not pry, Viola could not resist picking up the frame and turning it over.

What she saw almost made her drop it.

'Oh,' she cried, in shock, 'it is a photograph of Mama when she was young.'

Viola's hand was shaking as she took it over to the window to see it more clearly. The glass was dusty but, sure enough, it was the unmistakeable image of her mother, aged perhaps eighteen or nineteen. The same deep brown eyes that Viola had inherited stared out of the frame at her with a seriousness that belied her tender years.

'I wonder why this has been hidden away in an old cupboard,' she thought. 'Surely, if this was Aunt Mary's she would have it on display somewhere?'

Then, the thought struck her that perhaps it did not belong to Aunt Mary but to Uncle Hugo.

She dimly recalled a fragment of family conversation she had once overheard that her Mama had made Lord Wakefield's acquaintance before Aunt Mary.

Shaken, Viola put it back in its hiding place and returned to the dressing table.

She felt as if she had inadvertently seen something that she really should not have. But why did she feel like that? And why was a photo of her dear Mama hidden away as if it was shameful?

Her mind whirling, she was still dwelling upon her strange discovery when Mirupa came into the room to announce that dinner would be ready in ten minutes.

CHAPTER THREE

Viola did not say a word during dinner about her discovery and matters were not helped by the fact that, once or twice, she caught her uncle staring at her with a strange look on his face.

Immediately that dinner had finished, she made her excuses, saying that she was fatigued and retired to her room.

She felt incredibly tempted to open up the cupboard again, but she did not. Instead, she allowed Mirupa to retire for the night and put herself to bed.

Although exhausted from her long journey, she still found it difficult to sleep.

'I cannot believe that I am here,' she said to herself, as the sounds of the unfamiliar Indian night wafted into the room. 'And that photograph of Mama. Why has it been hidden in a cupboard as if it was something to be ashamed about?'

Eventually she drifted into a dream.

She dreamt that her mother was in the room, sitting on the end of her bed and telling her that everything would be all right.

It was so realistic that when Mirupa awoke her the next morning, she was convinced that it had all happened.

And then, with sinking heart, Viola remembered that her beloved Mama was no longer alive. She became so miserable that it was hard for her to get up.

She wept silently into the china bowl that Mirupa had filled with water for her.

'I must pull myself together,' she thought. 'I must not make Aunt Mary think that I am unhappy to be here. Besides, all my crying will not bring back Mama.'

She splashed her face with some more cold water and straightened the long sleeves on her black linen dress.

"I must ask Aunt Mary for some advice on suitable attire for this climate," she said to Mirupa, as they left the bedroom.

"Must you continue to wear black?" asked Mirupa.

"Oh, I do not think I could do that," replied Viola, wistfully, "it would seem disrespectful."

"Surely your parents would not mind? After all, you are in India."

"I shall have to give the matter more thought."

"Ah, Viola. I trust that you slept well?"

Aunt Mary's eyes lit up as Viola entered the dining room. Viola quickly noticed that Uncle Hugo was not present.

"Where is my uncle?" she asked, a little tentatively.

"He has gone to his office already – I am afraid you have missed him."

Viola sat down and was served tea. She cast her eyes along the table and saw strange fruits on platters.

"You must try the mango," suggested her aunt, pointing at some slices of deep-orange fruit, "it has a heavenly taste."

She signalled to Dinesh to place some on Viola's plate. It did, indeed, smell wonderful. Viola cut a piece with her knife and put it into her mouth. It melted on her tongue in a burst of flavour.

"Mmm, this is exquisite," cried Viola, savouring the rich juicy fruit.

"They grow on trees in the garden, Dinesh picked these himself."

"Why has uncle had to go so early today?" asked Viola between mouthfuls.

"Oh, it is this trying Russian question. I keep hoping that it will resolve itself, but they will insist on trying to capture land which is not theirs. There has been a report to the effect that a spy ship has been seen in the Gulf."

"I confess, I do find the situation a little alarming," admitted Viola. "I had no idea that there was this kind of problem here – "

"Otherwise you would not have come?" said her aunt, finishing her sentence.

Viola looked quite ashamed – had not her mother taught her not to show her emotions if they might offend?

Aunt Mary laughed and then continued,

"As I told you yesterday, we should not concern ourselves unduly. The Russians wish to seize control of parts of India, as it would benefit them tremendously, but we shall make sure that it does not happen.

"Hugo says that they are not moving as swiftly as they would like, as the mountains are difficult to negotiate. There is another perilous range of mountains that they will have to scale in order to pass through Afghanistan, so I think we are safe for quite some time yet. In any case, I have every confidence that the British Army can repel them before the situation becomes serious."

"And if it should?" asked Viola, tentatively. She felt a little worried that she had placed herself in some kind of danger by leaving the safety of home.

"That is why your uncle is working so hard at the

moment to ensure it does not happen. But, if things should become shall we say – uncertain – then we shall remove ourselves to Bombay at once. We still own a property there."

The conversation fell into a lull and Viola wanted to ask her why a picture of her Mama had been shut up in a cupboard, but for some reason, she could not.

She recalled her aunt's strange comment from the day before, when she had remarked at how it had not been easy to have a more beautiful younger sister.

Viola opened her mouth to say something, but Dinesh entered the room.

"*Memsahib*, the stables wish to know if you will need the carriage today."

"Thank you, Dinesh, I will require it after luncheon. Would you be good enough to ask Markyate to present himself at two o'clock?"

He bowed and left the room.

"Markyate?" asked Viola laughing, "that does not sound like an Indian name."

"You are quite correct," answered her aunt, "he came with us as groom and coachman when Hugo was first sent here. He is excellent with the horses and Hugo does not trust anyone else with his own mount. Napoleon is a very fine horse but highly strung. He will not allow anyone except Markyate and Hugo to touch him."

"He does sound exciting and may I visit the stables to see him?" asked Viola, her eyes shining with delight. This horse sounded like a challenge and she desperately wanted to see if Napoleon would allow her to ride him.

"I expected that you would ask such a question and so I will show you the house and grounds as soon as we have finished our meal."

Aunt Mary laid down her napkin and rang for some

more tea. Although it was only nine o'clock the heat was already quite considerable.

"And after luncheon, we shall be paying a call to the dress shop. Mrs. Patel is heavenly with a needle and will make you some more practical clothes. She saved my life with her cotton gowns. They are as light as a feather and are wonderfully cool and we shall also buy you some hats. The sun is fierce in these parts and I do not want you to get sunstroke."

As Viola finished her tea, the two of them sat in silence.

'Such an incredible country and so utterly different from anything I have been used to,' she thought to herself.

She could not imagine Cousin Agnes dealing with this heat. She fainted every year at the summer concerts in Hyde Park, claiming that it was too hot for her.

Her thoughts turned once more to the photograph.

'If only I could ask Aunt Mary – '

But before she had a chance to think any more about broaching the subject, Aunt Mary put down her tea cup with a decisive air and announced,

"If you are ready, Viola, I would like to show you around the house."

She showed her the elegant drawing room and the study where her uncle spent his time going through his dispatch boxes. A couple of them stood on the desk awaiting his attention.

"They are from Her Majesty's Government," explained Aunt Mary. "Your uncle is a very important man in India – he answers to the Viceroy and no one else."

As they passed the painting of the Georgian lady, Viola seized her chance.

"Tell me, aunt, who is that lady? She has the look of

our family about her."

"You are very clever to notice," replied Aunt Mary. "She is my Great-Aunt Caroline. That portrait used to hang in the house on the Isle of Wight. Although I did not wish to take responsibility for the estate, which is why your Mama took it, I did ask for the painting. Look closer – she has your eyes."

Viola blushed. Even though she had thought so herself, she had been too modest to make the observation.

"She is very beautiful," she remarked.

"Yes, isn't she."

"I am often told that I resemble Mama," said Viola, nervously, for she was aware of the fact that this topic of conversation was somewhat sensitive.

Her aunt gave her a searching look and moved quickly down the stairs.

"Come, I have left the best until the very last. The veranda and the gardens are my most favourite places."

'Now I am sure that there was some kind of rivalry between her and Mama,' thought Viola, as they walked through the French doors of the drawing room.

The veranda was painted white and ran all round the house. There were hanging baskets of vines and comfortable chairs everywhere.

"This is where I like to sit and read in the afternoons," said Aunt Mary.

"It looks heavenly," commented Viola, "are you not troubled by flies here?"

"Not terribly – I have one of the servants' children fan me. As Hugo and I were not fortunate enough to be blessed with a family, I love to have the young ones around me. They are all delightful and so happy."

Viola detected a hint of sadness in her voice. She was

coming to the conclusion that there were many pieces in her aunt's life that gave her cause for regret.

The gardens were utterly beautiful and Viola fell in love with them at once.

"Such strange and exotic plants!" she declared, fingering a large palm that waved high over her head.

"Much of what you see was already here before the house was built. We tried to grow a lawn but the climate is not favourable to green expanses of turf."

Viola turned around to view the house from the end of the garden where they now stood and was surprised to see a figure of a man coming down the path.

At first, she was concerned about this unannounced stranger, but as he drew closer, she could see by his uniform that he was in the Army – his brass buttons shone and the gold on his epaulettes told her that he held a high rank.

Shading her eyes, she could see how the sun made his russet-coloured hair gleam like fire.

"Who is this?" she asked, as the tall figure strode closer.

"Ah, it is Lord Devonport, such a charming young man. He must have dropped in to see Hugo."

The young man hailed them, a broad smile breaking out across his striking features.

"Over here," cried Aunt Mary, waving at him.

As soon as the Earl came nearer, Viola could see the reason for her aunt's coyness. He was very good-looking and in fact, Viola had never seen a more handsome man!

"You have come just in time to meet my niece. Viola, this is Lord Devonport. Charles, may I introduce Miss Viola Brookfield?"

The Earl shook Viola's hand and she was somewhat startled to find herself staring, not into a pair of blue eyes as she had expected, but startlingly green ones.

She had to look away quickly – they were such an incredible shade. She felt herself colouring. It had always been this way with Viola – she had often become shy in the presence of very good-looking people.

'My, he is a handsome man,' she thought, as she watched him take Aunt Mary's arm and walk around the fig trees with her.

"Charles is on a secret mission in Mandavi and he will not tell me what it is," exclaimed her aunt, almost girlishly. "I have been pleading with him to tell me what it is, but he will not divulge a single thing."

Viola was surprised to see her aunt behaving so flirtatiously as she laughed and looked up at the Earl in what could only be described as a coquettish fashion.

As she walked behind them towards the house, she admired his tall, broad-shouldered figure. She thought him rather dashing.

"You will, of course, have coffee with us on the veranda," invited Aunt Mary.

"I would be delighted," he replied, smiling at Viola and making her blush.

'I am such a goose,' thought Viola, 'he is only being pleasant and yet I cannot even meet his gaze.'

The Earl waited until she and her aunt had sat down and then he seated himself opposite Viola.

"Is this your first time in India?" he asked.

"Yes, it is," replied Viola, who was busy kicking herself that she could not think of something witty and amusing to say.

"And how are you finding it?"

"Rather bewildering," she answered and then hung her head as she could not bear his keen gaze.

"I imagine you must miss England and your family?"

"Viola's parents were both killed in an accident not so long ago," cut in Aunt Mary, upon seeing her niece's expression.

"Oh, I am so sorry," said the Earl, compassion filling his eyes.

"Thank you."

Viola could not think of a single interesting thing to say to this charming gentleman who was attempting to engage her in polite conversation.

'I wish I was not so tongue-tied,' she thought sadly, as her aunt and the Earl merrily chattered away about mutual acquaintances. 'I should like to know more about him, but how can I, if I am unable to form a single sentence?'

Dinesh appeared with the coffee and Aunt Mary made a great show of pouring a cup for the Earl.

"Viola was told to make your acquaintance by a mutual friend. You are familiar with Albie and Agnes Dawlish?"

"Why, of course. Dear old Albie. We have played cards together. Not for money, I hasten to add, and his sister, Agnes, is charming."

"They are my cousins," added Viola, pleased that she had found her tongue at last. "My father's brother's children."

"Then I would guess that you resemble your mother in looks and colouring – both Albie and Agnes are as dark as you are fair."

"That is true," replied Viola, "Papa's family are all dark but Mama's are fair."

"Then you have inherited the best of both with your blonde hair and brown eyes," remarked the Earl, in a low voice, still staring at her.

Viola blushed again and pressed her hand against her burning cheek.

"My dear, are you feeling unwell?" asked Aunt Mary with a concerned air.

"I am quite well, thank you, aunt. This coffee is delicious – I did not expect to be able to stomach a hot drink in this heat."

"Shall I call for Ravi and ask him to fan you?"

"No, aunt, that will not be necessary."

The conversation fell into a lull and Viola kept her eyes cast downwards, for each time that she looked up, the Earl was staring at her.

"You will, of course, dine with us tonight, Charles?"

Viola's heart skipped a beat. She very much wanted to spend more time getting to know this interesting young man.

"I would be delighted," he answered in his lively clear voice.

It was easy for Viola to imagine him giving orders to his men. He had an air of authority about him that was not entirely born out of his station in life.

"Then we shall expect you at half-past seven," said her aunt, ringing a small hand bell next to her to call one of the servants to show the Earl out.

"It has been a pleasure meeting you," he said, as he made a point of saying his goodbyes to Viola before her aunt.

Viola looked down and immediately told herself off for appearing too shy. Perhaps she was misreading the Earl's attentiveness and he was simply being charming. He certainly had a way with Aunt Mary.

The Earl bowed and left.

"Such a good-looking young man, don't you think?" said Aunt Mary, wistfully, as they watched his strong shoulders disappear into the house.

"He certainly seems very pleasant," agreed Viola.

"Oh," said her Aunt, suddenly, "I completely forgot to show you the stables. The Earl took my mind off it when we were in the garden."

"It really does not matter – I can see them later. Besides, I enjoyed the company of our visitor."

Although he had only just left, already Viola could not wait to see him again that evening.

*

After a light luncheon, the carriage was brought round to the front of the house and Viola noticed that it was an English servant who was in charge of the two fine horses. She assumed it must be Markyate.

The man was big and burly with a no-nonsense air about him. Although not as refined in manners as Dinesh or Morton, he appeared to know what he was doing.

He held open the door to the old-fashioned carriage and helped both ladies in.

"Goodness, these steps seem to get steeper each time I get into this thing," declared Aunt Mary, as she opened up her parasol.

"Perhaps if you ask Uncle Hugo nicely, he will buy you a new one. The latest phaetons back in London have slightly lower steps, aunt."

"No, no, your uncle will not hear of it. He does not like to spend money unnecessarily."

"Then perhaps a buggy? That would be lower on the road and not as expensive as a new phaeton."

"No, my dear, we could not be seen out in a buggy. That would never do. We have certain standards to maintain."

Viola thought it curious. She knew that her uncle was a rich man and she did not follow how standards could be maintained with such a creaking carriage.

She assumed that the newest fashions had not arrived on the Subcontinent and wondered what kind of dress shop they might be about to visit.

'I do hope that Mrs. Patel will not be thinking of running me up a crinoline,' she thought, horrified.

Viola was a young girl who loved nice clothes and, even though she was in mourning, her gowns were still attractive and the height of fashion.

"Ah, here we are."

The carriage drew up outside a rather unassuming building. Aunt Mary walked in through the open door with Viola following her. Viola gasped as she saw the bales of coloured cottons in every variety of vivid shades. Everywhere she looked were silks and chiffons, so fine that they were like wisps of cloud.

Two hours later, they emerged from the shop, with Markyate carrying several parcels and hatboxes.

"I would not be caught wearing such a hat in London," she exclaimed, tugging at the wide brim of her latest purchase.

"You will need it in India," said her aunt, "the sun is very fierce and a parasol is not always enough. Mrs. Patel will send your new gowns once they are finished. You will not be disappointed."

"I do hope that they are as nice as she has promised," replied Viola. "I feel quite daring ordering two in white."

"That is just in case you change your mind about wearing full mourning while you are here. You may find wearing black too oppressive in the hot weather. Mrs. Patel's cottons are as fine as gauze and you will undoubtedly bake in black."

Viola laughed. She had not been able to stop thinking

about the Earl of Devonport. As she selected the fabrics for her new dresses, she was thinking,

'Will the Earl find me pleasing in this dress? Will he think me attractive?'

She suddenly felt very tired and, as soon as they arrived back at the house, she informed her aunt that she wished to take a nap.

"It is the heat that makes you tired," suggested Aunt Mary, ringing for cold drinks, "have some *nimbu pani* and then you can rest awhile. Do not worry about wearing anything too grand for dinner tonight – it will be quite informal."

"But the Earl – " began Viola, anxiously. She wanted to make a good impression.

"Do not worry about Charles, he is used to our ways and knows that we do not always wear our best for dinner every evening."

Viola rather thought that she would like to do so, but did not say anything.

As she rose to retire upstairs, her uncle appeared in the doorway.

"Hugo!" exclaimed her aunt. "I did not know that you were home."

Lord Wakefield hovered in the doorway and did not seem anxious to linger.

"I had some dispatch boxes to go through."

"I have invited Charles for dinner, I hope that you do not mind – "

"Not at all. Splendid fellow!" he replied. "He did stop by my office to tell me that he was dining with us tonight, so I came home early so that I might finish my work in time to dine with you all. Now, if you will excuse me, I have much to do."

Viola watched him from the top of the stairs as he walked into his study and closed the door behind him.

'I am certain that there is some mystery in this house,' she thought, as she walked to her room, 'and I intend to find out what it is.'

*

In her room, Mirupa was waiting and had drawn a bath for her.

Afterwards Viola took a nap and awoke in time to dress for dinner. She wished that one of her new gowns had been ready, but even the lightning fingers of Mrs. Patel could not perform miracles.

She selected a becoming black satin dress that had a great many jet beads sewn into it.

'Oh, I am so tired of wearing mourning,' she declared at her reflection in the cheval mirror as Mirupa laced her into the bodice.

By the time that Viola was ready, she was feeling nervous. She had heard the front door bell ring and reckoned that the Earl had arrived.

Flushed with excitement, she ran downstairs and through the open door of the drawing room she could see the Earl, sherry in hand, chatting to her uncle.

As she approached, he looked up and an expression of pure pleasure crossed his face.

"How very lovely you look this evening, Miss Brookfield."

"Thank you," she replied, wishing that she could ask him to call her Viola.

"I trust that you have had an amusing day?"

"Yes, thank you."

Once again, Viola cursed herself for being tongue-tied in his presence. It was certainly unusual for her.

When Dinesh entered to announce that dinner was ready, the Earl offered Viola his arm.

Blushing, she took it and thrilled secretly to his warmth. She was very innocent and had only ever been heavily chaperoned at meetings with young men. She had only ever been kissed once and had not found it to her liking.

Yet, there was something about the Earl that both unnerved and thrilled her.

She shocked herself by wondering what it might be like to kiss his firm lips.

Viola was still reeling from her unexpected thoughts when they sat down to dinner and she felt that she could not eat a morsel.

Even though the food was delicious, she was far too aware of the Earl's presence. So much so that halfway through the meal, her aunt asked her if she was feeling well.

"Thank you, but I am rather tired, it must be the heat that is affecting my appetite."

Dinesh took away her untouched plate of lamb cutlets without remark.

"I was very much the same when I first arrived in Mandavi," said the Earl, trying to put her at her ease, "but within a month or so, I recovered my zest for food. Might I suggest that little and often is the best course of action?"

Viola smiled thinly at him.

'He will think me so dull,' she said to herself, 'and without any kind of interesting conversation.'

There were no cigars after the meal. Instead, Dinesh brought round a decanter of brandy. Viola refused a glass and moved on to her coffee.

"You aunt tells me that you enjoy riding," said the Earl.

Instantly, Viola lit up. This was one topic of

conversation where she could more than hold her own.

"Yes, that is true and I was very disappointed not to have seen the stables today. Aunt Mary kept me so busy that there was very little time. However, I am looking forward to viewing them tomorrow."

"You are in for a treat as Hugo boasts some of the finest mounts in the whole of Gujarat."

"I have heard much about this Napoleon and I am keen to meet him."

Her uncle laughed from the other end of the table,

"Don't let his quiet manner lead you into thinking that he's a lamb. Once saddled – that is, if you can get a saddle on the devil – he's as wild as the wind!"

"As twice as fast, I hear," added the Earl, "although I have never been able to handle him, let alone mount him."

"That is because he knows he has only one master," said Lord Wakefield.

"I should like to try and ride him," piped up Viola, suddenly, much to everyone's surprise.

"Dear, you could not do that. He would surely kill you!" cried her aunt.

Her uncle stared at Viola for a long moment yet again and there was something in his gaze that unnerved her. Was he thinking of her Mama, who had outraged everyone by riding bareback on the feistiest horse in the family stables?

"If Viola wishes to try, then she is welcome," he said, in a low voice that betrayed his emotion by trembling. "That is – if Markyate allows her anywhere near his beloved Napoleon. He treats that horse as if it was his son. Now come, Dinesh has arranged for more coffee to be served on the veranda."

He rose and took his glass of brandy with him and Aunt Mary followed him.

However, the Earl lingered, waiting for Viola to leave the table.

"Might I take the liberty of asking you to accompany me on a ride tomorrow afternoon?" he asked, somewhat nervously.

Viola could hardly believe what he was asking her. She felt certain that she had bored him to tears all evening.

"Y-yes," she stammered, thrilled to her core.

"Wonderful. Then I shall call for you at five o'clock."

He smiled at her and the corners of his eyes crinkled.

Later on the veranda, Aunt Mary sat down next to Viola in a confidential manner.

"Dearest, Charles seems to be rather taken with you," she whispered, as the Earl and Uncle Hugo discussed the Russian crisis, "such an eligible young man. Any young lady would count herself very fortunate indeed to have his suit."

"Oh, aunt, he has only asked me to go riding with him, not to marry him!"

"All in good time, my dear, all in good time."

Aunt Mary smiled to herself and drank her coffee, while Viola's mind raced. *Marriage!* She had never even considered a romance, yet here was her aunt, imagining all kinds of nonsense.

'I must not see what is not there,' Viola told herself, much later when she had said goodbye to the Earl and retired to bed. 'Aunt Mary is far too romantic – she has been reading too many novels.'

Even so, she could not help dreaming of the Earl and wonder what the next afternoon would bring –

CHAPTER FOUR

Viola awoke the next morning feeling as if she had not rested in the least. She had hardly slept at all and felt very impatient for five o'clock to come so that she could see the Earl again.

"A whole nine hours before he calls," she sighed to her reflection, as Mirupa combed out her hair.

"Do not wish the day away, there is so much to see and enjoy in Mandavi that there are not enough hours in the day. Have you been to the ruined temple in the jungle yet?"

"No," exclaimed Viola, with her eyes widening, "it sounds most interesting. Where is it?"

"It is to the North of Mandavi – I am certain that Dinesh would be able to tell you the way because I know that he has visited it many times."

"Perhaps I shall ask the Earl to take me there when we go for our ride late this afternoon," said Viola, thinking aloud and quite forgetting that Mirupa was present.

Mirupa giggled and asked rather mischievously,

"So is that why *memsahib* is so keen for the hours to pass?"

Immediately, Viola flushed deep red. How silly of her to be so candid in front of a servant. Did they not gossip at every opportunity?

"Do not worry – your secret is safe with me," said Mirupa, appearing to read her mind. "He is very handsome, is he not? We do not see hair that colour very often in this country. There are mountain people in the North with reddish hair, but not the colour of copper like his Lordship's."

The two girls looked at each other and burst out laughing.

Viola was glad to have found a friendly female to make small talk with. She had not counted on quite how lonely she was going to feel without young friends around and although Mirupa could not be considered as a friend, Viola did think it wonderful to be able to chatter girlishly with her.

Later, over breakfast, Aunt Mary informed Viola that she had arranged for them to visit a friend of hers, Lady Armitage, for tea that morning.

"She has a niece who is around your age staying with her," she told Viola. "I have not met her, but perhaps she would be good company for you. You need to have young people around you, Viola, not us old ones."

"Aunt Mary, I enjoy being with you and it is helping me with my grief over Mama and Papa. After all, you knew them both so well and I am certain that there is much you can tell me about them that I do not already know."

Viola was aware that her comments had as much to do with finding out the secret behind the mysterious photograph as discovering more about her parents.

"Oh, what is there to tell, darling? They were both wonderful people who were lucky enough to find each other and then their life was cruelly cut short."

"But I know little of Mama's life before she was married and I long to hear what she was like as a child – "

Aunt Mary put down her teacup with a sigh.

"She was adorable and so pretty that everyone who saw her fell in love with her. In spite of what you may believe, I wish I knew more about your Papa, but the Brookfields are an odd lot and I do believe that your Papa was the only decent one."

Viola was quite shocked as, although she had met very few of her father's side of the family, she had never heard anything negative about them.

"Now, come along, Viola, it is time to see the horses. The Earl will be on his own mount today, but we should ask Markyate to select a suitable one for you."

She could not wait to meet the infamous Napoleon. She craned her neck to see along the row of stable doors, hoping for a glimpse of him.

"This is my horse, Misty," said Aunt Mary, stroking a dappled grey mare.

"She is beautiful and who is that fine animal in the next stable?"

"That is Snowball, she looks as if she doesn't care for anything but eating, but she flies like the wind. Perhaps Markyate will select her for your ride – she is quite wilful, but a darling nevertheless."

"Hello, girl," crooned Viola, patting her forelock. "Aren't you beautiful?"

The mare snorted and pushed her large nose into Viola's hand.

"No, I do not have anything nice for you to eat, but perhaps later – "

"And this, is Napoleon!" announced Aunt Mary, as Markyate led a huge black stallion towards one of the stalls.

The horse was snorting noisily and held his head high in full knowledge that he was the most handsome creature in the place.

"What a proud beast!" cried Viola, eyeing him appreciatively, "and such a fine profile. Markyate, would I be allowed to ride him?"

"I don't think he'll be letting anyone apart from your uncle near him, miss, he can be dangerous if you don't know how to handle him."

"Come, Viola, it is time we made our way to Lady Armitage's house," interrupted Aunt Mary. "Markyate, is the carriage ready?"

"Yes, my Lady."

Viola could not help but steal a few backward glances at Napoleon. He was as black as night and she could see how highly strung he was.

'How I should love to ride him,' she thought as she followed her aunt.

Twenty minutes later, Viola found herself in the carriage with her aunt, en route to Lady Armitage's.

"Do not take offence if she is a little cool with you, Viola," explained Aunt Mary. "Lady Armitage is one of the few friends I have here from home, but I am well aware that she thinks it is she and not Queen Victoria who is Empress of India!"

Viola could not help but laugh. She had met similar grand old ladies in London who behaved as if they were Royalty and she knew what she had to do.

"Do not worry, aunt, I shall smile and be utterly charming as well as mute, with no opinion of my own."

"I wonder what Millicent will be like? I do hope she might be a suitable friend for you."

"I am quite used to amusing myself, but it is very kind of you to think of me."

"And if she is not," continued her aunt, ignoring what Viola had said, "we shall give a ball and invite many guests.

That is, unless you feel that it would be not correct in view of the fact that we are both, strictly speaking, in mourning."

"Aunt, Mama loved balls as much as anyone and I do not think that she or Papa in Heaven would be frowning at us for enjoying ourselves."

"Yes, you are right. But, nevertheless, if you feel that you do not wish to dance and make merry, I am certain that everyone will understand. Ah, here we are."

They had drawn up outside a huge set of gates.

The house was magnificent and its veranda was even larger than the Wakefield's.

They were shown into a lavishly decorated morning room in which Lady Armitage was already seated on a silk covered sofa. She was large and white-haired with tremendous jowls.

On a chair nearby, sat a young girl with a round face and curly mouse coloured hair. She was busy preening herself, tugging at the curls that sprang over her forehead and looked at Viola with a boldly appraising stare.

"Lady Armitage, how nice to see you."

Aunt Mary kissed the old lady on the cheek and sat down on a comfortable chair. Viola was shown to a rather hard looking red velvet covered wooden one.

"This is my niece, Miss Viola Brookfield. She has come to stay with us after both her parents were tragically killed."

"I am so sorry, Miss Brookfield, but spend a month in India and you will have soon forgotten your woes. This is a wild country with unbelievable poverty – and I have to say, they have only themselves to blame."

Viola looked quite shocked at her pronouncement and quickly ascertained the kind of views that Lady Armitage might hold. She decided to say very little, as she had planned, for fear of causing offence with her contrary views.

"This is my niece, Miss Millicent Armitage," said Lady Armitage, waving her hand at the girl with the curly hair.

Viola nodded at her, but had already decided that she did not care for Miss Armitage one jot.

"I do not think that we have met in London, have we?" asked Millicent with a superior air.

"I believe not," replied Viola, coolly.

"My aunt tells me that you are a cousin of Agnes – so you must know Charles?

Viola looked at her uncomprehendingly.

"Charles?"

"Oh, you probably know him as Lord Devonport. We are terribly good friends – rather close even."

Viola was quite taken aback by the girl referring to the Earl in such a casual manner. She wanted to ask her how she knew him, but did not wish to seem at all interested. Even so, she felt more than a little unnerved. What was she to the Earl?

"Yes, I have met him twice," replied Viola after a long pause.

"Oh, Charles is a simply wonderful man," gushed Millicent, rolling her eyes, "and such a dear, dear friend. He's terribly high up in the Army, you know."

"Yes, so my aunt and uncle tell me," answered Viola, trying to be polite.

"Charles is so brave and involved in some awfully secret business to do with the Russkies. I am certain that I would be terrified if I came across one of them, but he chases them off all the time."

From then on, Millicent took every opportunity to rub in the fact that she was 'good friends' with the Earl.

Viola tried not to take the bait, but her heart sank with each successive boast.

"So where are your people from?" asked Lady Armitage, cutting into Millicent mid sentence.

"Mama and Papa owned a house in Connaught Square and a house on the Isle of Wight that Mama inherited from her great-aunt."

"Brookfield, Brookfield – no, I do not recall any Brookfields in Connaught Square, are you certain that is where they lived?"

Viola could not believe her ears. Was the woman casting doubt on her?

"Yes, quite certain. I myself now own the house as well as the one at Cowes."

"Then you are a most fortunate young lady. You must be on your guard against bounders who would marry you for your property. Plenty of them around."

"Oh, but they are all in love with *me*," interjected Millicent. "It is such a nuisance to be pestered, morning, noon and night."

Viola did not reply. She looked at the clock but it was still only ten minutes past eleven – how much longer would she have to sit here and listen to Lady Armitage's snobbery and Millicent's self aggrandisement?

The hands of the clock crawled slowly and Viola thought that she would die from boredom. She became annoyed by the only topic of Millicent's conversation – '*Charles*'.

So she was much relieved when, at a quarter to twelve, Aunt Mary announced that they had to leave.

"Such a pity," exclaimed Lady Armitage.

"We shall be having a ball soon and I do hope you will both join us."

"I would love to," jumped in Millicent, before her aunt could open her mouth, "I have just bought a new ball gown and I am longing to wear it."

As they rose to depart, Millicent came over to Viola.

"You really should not have gone to so much effort for us," she said, in a confidential tone whilst eyeing Viola's black silk dress. "In India, one does not dress as if for dinner during the day, you know. It's considered frightfully overdone."

She said it with a sly smile, knowing that her hard-of-hearing aunt would not catch what she was saying and tick her off.

Viola gave the girl a cool look and did not reply. She was determined that she was not going to show the awful creature the slightest sign of being offended.

Outside in the carriage, Aunt Mary sighed heavily and patted Viola's hand.

"I am so sorry to have put you through such an ordeal. I had no idea that Millicent would be so full of herself, but I did know that Lady Armitage always asks about one's family when first she meets someone. It is as if she is interviewing servants, rather than getting acquainted."

"Millicent made some catty comment to the effect that I was overdressed."

Aunt Mary waved her hand as if to dismiss the idea.

"Stuff and nonsense! You should dress attractively no matter what the weather or where you are. India is far more informal than London, I'll grant you, but some of us have standards that we like to maintain."

Viola felt secretly pleased that her aunt had not thought much of Millicent – she did not mention her constant dropping of the Earl's name, although she was certain that her aunt would have noticed it.

The Earl – how Viola could not wait to see him again.

The hours after luncheon dragged by and even though she tried to rest later, she was far too excited.

Mirupa had pressed her riding habit and it was now hanging from the wardrobe. Viola lay on the bed, looking at it and wishing that it was time to put it on.

She tried reading, but, try as she might, she could not concentrate.

Her aunt was having an afternoon nap and the house was as quiet as a Church.

Viola crept downstairs and saw that there was yet another pile of dispatch boxes waiting outside her uncle's study.

She stroked the red leather and the brass locks. They filled her with curiosity, but she knew that she must not be tempted to try to open them.

Instead, she wandered around the house, looking at every last ornament and painting in minute detail.

'I wonder if the Earl really is as close to Millicent as she has made out,' she mused. 'I have to discover if she is a rival for his affections.'

Viola surprised herself by even thinking such a thought, but if she was not interested in him, why did she feel such utter panic at the thought that he might be keen on Millicent?

At four o'clock, after idling around on the veranda and taking yet another turn around the garden, Viola went back upstairs to get ready.

Never before had she taken such care with her appearance.

'I want to look as attractive as I possibly can,' she thought, as Mirupa helped her into her ankle-length skirt and linen blouse.

Just before five, she was downstairs breathlessly waiting for the jangle of the front door bell.

She did not have to wait long for the Earl was a punctual man.

Taking a deep breath, Viola, waited while Dinesh opened the door. As he did so, she saw the Earl standing there with a smile on his handsome face.

"Good afternoon, Miss Brookfield," he said, raising his cap. He was still wearing his Army uniform and the brass buttons glittered in the late afternoon sun.

"I hope that you are ready? Markyate is bringing a horse round for you."

Viola stepped outside and admired the Earl's own mount – a massive, chestnut stallion with a thick black mane.

"What is his name?" she asked, admiring the horse as the boy held the lead.

"Jasper," replied the Earl, proudly, "and look – here is your horse. I do believe that Markyate had already selected one for you before I came."

"That is correct. Aunt Mary and I visited the stables this morning and she said that she thought he would choose Snowball."

"I think it is a good choice – a beautiful woman should ride a beautiful horse."

Although blushing Viola was extremely pleased.

'He thinks I am beautiful,' she thought, incredulously, as he helped her on to Snowball's back.

She watched as the Earl mounted Jasper. He made it look effortless and seemed utterly at home sat on his horse. Viola thought it suited him.

"Now, where would you like to go, Miss Brookfield?"

"Mirupa, my maid, mentioned that there is a most

interesting ruined temple to the North of Mandavi. Do you know it?"

"I am afraid not – that will have to wait for another day, but I do know of a lovely Palace that overlooks the Gulf of Kutch that you may care to see. It belongs to the Duke of Morpeth. I am certain that your aunt will know him."

"Oh, I do not think we should call without an appointment," said Viola, "it would not be correct."

The Earl smiled at her and then answered,

"I quite agree and so we shall content ourselves with just looking at his house. It is a good few miles away and the scenery is superb. I think you will enjoy it."

"Then, lead the way."

They set off down the driveway and proceeded through Mandavi town to the outskirts. Once clear of the last few houses, the Earl urged Jasper into a gallop.

They rode for a while before pausing at the top of a hill to admire the view. The landscape was quite unlike any Viola had ever seen.

"Look, you can see the shoreline from here," called the Earl.

"Is it true that there have been Russian spy ships seen in the Gulf?"

"Yes, that is right, I myself once led a sortie to chase a yacht out of the bay."

"Was that not a dangerous assignment?"

"It was, but my men are more than a match for a few Russians," declared the Earl with pride.

"Is it true that they are gaining ground as each week passes?"

The Earl looked off into the distance before he answered and Viola realised that she had asked him a sensitive question.

"I know your uncle is worried about the outbreaks of rioting. The Russians are certainly stirring up a lot of trouble in the villages around Mandavi. How they are infiltrating past our lines we do not know, but they are creating problems."

"Heavens! I did not realise that they were actually in Mandavi. Why have they not been arrested?"

"Do not panic, Miss Brookfield. The Russians who are at large are no more than spies. They are not armed or fighting men and they are only here to cause trouble and to upset the natives."

"And the Russians in the Bay?"

"Ah, they are a different matter, but I am not allowed to make further comment. Suffice to say that they are probably looking to see where they can breach our lines with a view to attempting a proper military landing."

"And do you think that might happen?"

"Highly unlikely. The bulk of the Russian Army is still fighting its way through the mountains of Turkistan – and then they have the most treacherous passes in the Subcontinent to negotiate."

"That is what Aunt Mary said."

"She is very well informed. Your uncle would be well aware of the current situation naturally."

"Aunt Mary says we will leave for Bombay if the Russians come too close"

"She is wise to have plans in place. None of us knows when the threat might become real, but at the moment, you have no cause to lose sleep. Now, shall we head for the shore? The house is best seen from the beach."

The Earl had given Viola much food for thought. Yes, it was all true and she was frightened, but if the Earl was involved in keeping the Russians at bay, it made her feel safer.

'He is so strong and capable,' she thought, as she raced to keep up with Jasper. 'I cannot imagine him being afraid of anything.'

Viola admired the way that he handled Jasper. She could see that the powerful stallion was not an easy horse to ride, perhaps as challenging as Napoleon and yet, the Earl made it seem as if he was riding a docile pony.

At last, they reached the long beach. Viola loved the sea and this stretch of water was no different. She dismounted and ran down to the shore.

The Earl followed and was soon by her side.

"See that promontory over there?" he said, pointing over to their left, "beyond that lies Arabia. That is where the Russians are sneaking their ships through."

"It looks such a long way away," said Viola, shielding her eyes from the sun.

"It is, but to a determined Russian spy ship, it is no distance at all."

Viola felt a shiver run through her body. She had never met a Russian and she wondered what they might look like. From what her aunt said, she had visions of rough cruel men who would not hesitate to commit acts of violence.

"But come, look at the beautiful scenery. And there is the Duke's house."

Viola turned to where the Earl was pointing. Hidden amongst dense foliage, the house was indeed magnificent and its rolling gardens almost reached the beach.

"I would very much like to see inside one day," remarked Viola, as they walked back towards their horses.

"Perhaps you shall. The Duke is a close friend of mine and I will introduce you. I believe that he has a daughter who is roughly your age."

Viola smiled. She hoped that the Duke's daughter was

nothing like the awful Millicent. *Millicent.* Why, she had quite forgotten to ask the Earl about her.

As they mounted, Viola casually said,

"I met someone earlier today who is a very good friend of yours."

"Oh, really? Is he a member of my garrison?"

Viola laughed. Either the Earl was playing the innocent or Millicent had exaggerated her bond of closeness with him.

"It is not a he, but a she. Millicent Armitage – Lady Armitage's niece?"

He thought for a moment and then asked,

"Would she be a curly-haired girl, much given to idle chatter?"

"That sounds like Millicent."

"Ah, yes," said the Earl, with a slightly exasperated look on his face. "Miss Armitage – "

Taking up his reins, he made no further comment.

'I do believe that Millicent is not the bosom friend that she makes herself out to be,' considered Viola, rather pleased.

It only strengthened her resolve to get to know the Earl better.

Viola wished with all her heart that their ride would not come to an end, but all too soon the Earl suggested that they turn their horses back towards the town.

"Will you stay to dinner? I am certain that Aunt Mary would be delighted to see you," asked Viola hopefully.

"I am sorry but I have a prior engagement," answered the Earl, without offering any further explanation.

"Oh," said Viola, disappointed.

"Come, it is getting late – your aunt will not be pleased

if I bring you back after dark."

'He suddenly seems so distant,' thought Viola, as they galloped down the dusty road. 'As if he has something or someone else on his mind. I do hope that he is not dining with the Armitages tonight.'

The thought troubled her a great deal and she wondered if his vagueness about Millicent had been feigned.

By the time that they reached her aunt's house, it was almost six-thirty. Markyate was waiting for her by the front porch and seemed relieved.

"I thought you'd both been kidnapped by bandits or Russians," he grunted, as he took Snowball's bridle.

"We went to the beach," said Viola, as the groom helped her dismount.

"Your aunt has been asking for you," said Markyate as he led Snowball back to the stables. The Earl remained mounted as Jasper impatiently pawed the ground.

Just then, Aunt Mary appeared in the doorway.

"You have returned. I was beginning to worry," she said, clutching at her throat. "Your uncle still has not yet returned."

The Earl was scanning the distance. His green eyes squinting against the sun.

"Look. Is that not his carriage approaching?"

In the distance Viola could see her uncle's carriage as it sped towards them.

"He seems in a terrible hurry," commented the Earl. "See how the coachman is driving those horses."

It crossed Viola's mind that something was wrong.

As soon as the carriage drew up the drive, her uncle could be seen, hanging out of the window and shouting at the top of his voice,

"Lord Devonport! You are urgently required."

"What can it be?" muttered Aunt Mary, fearfully.

"There has been an uprising in Chindee and the Earl is needed at once. Come, there is no time to lose!"

The Earl did not hesitate. He spurred Jasper into action and with a nod towards Viola and Aunt Mary rode off down the driveway

"Hugo. Do be careful," cried Aunt Mary, as the carriage followed the Earl.

"Oh, Aunt Mary! What is happening?" asked Viola. "What is all this about an uprising?"

"It's the Russians," she replied grimly. "They will be at the bottom of this."

Viola was thinking only of the Earl – suppose he was killed? She had heard tales of riots in the villages and when there was unrest in India, the Army suppressed it efficiently. If the Russians were involved, perhaps it would not be so easy to quell?

'Oh, Charles,' she thought, as she watched her uncle's carriage disappear – the Earl had long since vanished as his horse was much faster. '*Please* be careful.'

Aunt Mary watched her niece closely, taking in her worried expression. After a while, she spoke,

"You appear to like the Earl very much, my dear," she said quietly.

Viola blushed deeply and did not reply.

'*It is true*, it is true,' she thought, as they walked into the house arm in arm.

She knew, deep down inside, that she could not deny the feelings that had begun to spring up in her heart –

CHAPTER FIVE

Dinner was not served that evening. Almost as soon as they had set foot in the dining room, Aunt Mary decided that she had little appetite and Viola concurred.

So Anjali was given the night off and both Viola and her aunt sat in the drawing room reading and sewing.

"We should not sit here and worry," sighed Aunt Mary.

"Chindee is only five miles away, is it not?"

"Yes, it is. Which is why this particular uprising is so unsettling. There have been riots before, but if the Earl has been called in, it must be quite serious."

"And you believe the Russians to be behind it?"

"I think that it is highly likely that they have a hand in it," replied Aunt Mary, resuming her sewing.

'Oh, Charles. Charles,' prayed Viola, silently, 'you *must* keep yourself safe.'

All she could think of was the Earl and the thought that she might lose him filled her with dread. If she was to be honest with herself, she would be forced to admit that the prospect of losing her uncle was far less alarming.

Her aunt looked up from her work to see that Viola was staring into space.

"Do not worry yourself about the Earl, my dear," she said, "he is more than capable of taking care of himself. He is a highly trained Officer who has seen a great deal of conflict in this country."

Viola was relieved that she did not have to hide her feelings from her aunt.

After all, had she not guessed – almost before Viola realised it herself – that she harboured feelings for the Earl?

"Then, I shall try not to fret. In fact, I think I shall now retire for the evening."

"Will you wake me if there is any news?" she asked, kissing her aunt.

"Only if it is necessary," she answered, "and God willing, you will be left to sleep undisturbed."

*

The day had been so tiring that Viola fell asleep as soon as her head hit the pillow.

However, in the early hours of the morning she was awakened by the sound of voices in the hall downstairs.

'Charles,' she thought, pulling on her dressing gown and running to the stairs.

Peering down over the banister, she could hear her aunt and uncle talking, but there was no sign of the Earl.

"Was it a terrible to-do?" said her aunt.

"Bloody, I'm afraid, my dear," replied her uncle. "Some of the natives were killed – it could not be helped."

"Oh," cried her aunt, "that is terribly unfortunate. And the Earl?"

Viola strained her ears at the mention of his name. Her heart was beating so hard that she could feel it through the cotton of her nightgown.

"He has sent his division back to the barracks and will be interrogating the captives this evening. I do not expect the poor chap will have any sleep tonight."

Viola sighed with relief – he was safe and unharmed!

She crept back to her room and slept fitfully, her dreams full of images of injured Indians.

*

Aunt Mary allowed Viola to sleep in. As a result, it was nearly ten o'clock before she opened her eyes.

She stretched and cast a glance towards the clock on the mantelpiece.

"Goodness! Look at the time. Why did Mirupa not call me?"

Jumping out of bed, Viola noticed that Mirupa had left a jug of water for her and some fruit in a dish.

'Aunt Mary must have asked her to let me sleep in,' she told herself.

Ten minutes later, Mirupa entered carrying a tea tray.

"How are you feeling today?" she asked.

"Very well, thank you, Mirupa. Is my aunt downstairs?"

"Yes, *memsahib,* and she has already gone out in her carriage. She said to tell you that she was delivering invitations to the dinner and ball."

"She must have decided to go ahead, despite the events in Chindee last night."

"It was a terrible affair at Chindee. Many were killed and wounded."

"I do hope that none of your friends or relatives were hurt?" asked Viola, remembering that Mirupa lived locally.

"No, but my brother could easily have been involved. He is rather anti-British, I am ashamed to say, and is a silly hothead at the best of times."

Viola was shocked. She did not know that there was strong anti-British feeling in India, having been brought up to believe that the British had been the saviours of India and had delivered them from a state of darkness.

"I do not understand why he should feel that way," she said quietly, "after all the British have done for India."

"There are some who feel that not all the changes have been for the good of the people, *memsahib*. My brother is one of them. Now, if you will excuse me, I have to run to Mrs. Patel's shop to pick up your new dresses."

"Oh, yes, I had quite forgotten about them," said Viola, somewhat distractedly, as Mirupa had given her much food for thought.

'I shall ask the Earl about this when I see him,' she said to herself, as Mirupa left the room. 'Perhaps he can explain it all to me.'

By the time that Mirupa returned, an hour later, Viola had eaten her breakfast and taken a turn around the garden before the sun became too hot.

The jasmine and gardenias were in bloom and a wonderful scent filled the air.

Viola watched as the buggy carrying Mirupa made its way up the drive.

She was so looking forward to seeing her new dresses, so she ran towards the front door in time to see her getting out, while a small boy helped her with the parcels.

"Mirupa," she called. "Please take them upstairs, I cannot wait to try them."

Five minutes later Viola was eagerly opening cardboard boxes.

"Oh, how pretty," she gasped, holding up a black cotton dress that was as light as a feather.

"Here are the two white dresses, *memsahib*," said Mirupa, without making any comment.

"I wish I had asked Mrs. Patel to make me a ball

gown," sighed Viola on seeing the beautiful and subtle embroidery that had been worked into the dresses.

"There is still time, *memsahib*. If I run back to the shop, I could order something special for you. Mrs. Patel has your measurements and if I told her that it is for a special occasion, she will oblige."

Viola thought for a few moments.

"Very well," she said, at last. "Ask her for something in lavender – that would be quite permissible in the circumstances. I will leave the details up to Mrs. Patel."

"You will be the most beautiful lady present, I promise you," Mirupa enthused, as she ran out of the room to fulfil her errand.

Viola hurriedly changed into one of her new gowns. Looking at her reflection in the cheval mirror, she very much liked what she saw.

The design was extremely flattering to her slender figure and it almost felt as if she was wearing gossamer rather than cotton.

'It may not be the height of Paris fashion,' she mused, 'but I think that it is still highly becoming.'

Viola wondered what the Earl might think of her in it. She was already planning to make an impression upon him at the ball the following week.

Aunt Mary returned for luncheon and was full of excitement about all the arrangements.

"So many people have confirmed their attendance," she trilled, as they moved towards the dining room. "I would not normally go out and personally deliver the invitations, but I wanted to make certain that everyone would come."

"Is Lady Armitage coming?" asked Viola, a little nervously.

"She is and, I am afraid, so is that dreadful niece of

hers. I am sorry, Viola, but I was put in an awkward position as Millicent was there when I arrived."

"It does not matter, aunt. I shall be polite but will not seek out her company."

Viola hesitated – she wanted to ask her aunt if the Earl was attending but could not bring herself to do so.

As if reading her mind, Aunt Mary smiled,

"And yes, Lord Devonport has accepted. He asked me to send his regards and to inform you that he is fine and well after the little altercation yesterday."

"I am most happy to hear the news," replied Viola, feeling relieved.

They sat down for luncheon. Aunt Mary continued to chatter away.

"We shall have a five-course dinner followed by dancing. It is important that we provide our guests with something to divert their minds from the awful events that are happening around us."

"When I spoke to Mirupa, she told me that the natives were not happy with the changes that the British have brought to India. She mentioned her brother – "

"Ah, yes, I believe that he has been something of an insurgent in the past. Most unfortunate, but we British have brought order to a chaotic nation and then all they do to thank us is to rebel like so many naughty children!"

Viola did not contradict her aunt, but she did not feel at all easy with the notion of one nation taking over the rule of another 'for its own good'.

'Perhaps I am not in full possession of the facts,' she told herself, 'and I have always been brought up not to argue with my elders and betters.'

For sure she would not have dared bring the subject up with her uncle. Although a fair man, he seemed certain of the righteousness of his position and, even though they had not discussed the topic, she knew already what his views might be.

"My new gowns arrived from Mrs. Patel this morning," began Viola, eager to change the conversation. "I am wearing one now."

"And most becoming it is, too," agreed Aunt Mary with a smile, "and did I not tell you that Mrs. Patel is a marvel?"

"I have asked Mirupa to order a new ball gown for me in lavender," added Viola, hesitantly.

"Very sensible," replied her aunt.

Viola was relieved that her aunt had not made a comment about her move away from deep mourning.

As she lingered, she wished with all her heart that the Earl would appear, just as he had on that first day she had met him, walking along the garden path.

But he was occupied with his mission and the Russians.

Viola shivered when she thought of Russian spies infiltrating Mandavi and, maybe, wandering around the town.

'Surely they would be noticed?' she asked herself.

*

Over the next few days, Viola tried not to dwell upon politics and instead threw herself into the preparations for the ball.

There was so much to do. Flowers to be ordered, food to be prepared and the whole of the house had to be cleaned from top to bottom. Aunt Mary had even booked a Viennese ensemble who travelled around India playing at balls.

When she was not occupied with the preparations, Viola took every opportunity she could to go out riding and explore the surrounding countryside.

Her aunt made her promise that she would not stray too far from Mandavi, although Viola had ridden right along the coast on her own. She loved the wild scenery and the mangroves and she never failed to thrill when she saw a huge elephant dragging logs or carrying its *mahout* to some ceremonial occasion.

She did not see the Earl in the days leading up to the ball. He had been most occupied with his duty and she was worried that he would not appear at all.

She thought about him constantly and wished she could find some excuse to go and see him.

But her aunt had cautioned her against appearing too eager and pointed out that girls like Millicent did not catch their men by doing all the chasing.

"It is common to pursue a gentleman," pronounced Aunt Mary, as she put the finishing touches to the menu.

"I know you are right, but he does not seem to be taking the initiative."

"Be patient, dearest. A gentleman such as the Earl has far more important matters to occupy himself with and love often has to take second place."

No matter what her aunt said, Viola was still impatient to see him again and thought that the day of the ball would never come.

But at last, it did.

She was awakened very early by the sound of chattering voices and a commotion beneath her window.

Her room overlooked the gardens, so the kitchen door was not far away. As she looked out of the window, she could see that a cart laden with fruit and vegetables had pulled up outside.

A bullock rather than a horse pulled it and the driver

seemed to be having an argument with Anjali the cook.

Viola yawned and pulled on her dressing gown. She knew that Mirupa would be going to pick up her new dress and she was feeling quite nervous.

Would the neckline be too daring for mourning and what about the sleeves?

Breakfast was rushed as Aunt Mary was constantly interrupted by servants, asking her advice or opinion, or informing her that such-and-such an item had arrived.

"Oh, this is all too much," she cried, as the message came that the ensemble had been delayed.

The day flew by and, very soon, Viola found that it was time for her to dress. Mirupa had the bath filled and then added some oil of sandalwood.

After the bath, she stood and brushed her hair until it shone and then put it up on Viola's head in an elaborate style.

Viola regarded her reflection in the mirror. The dress was most becoming and she was extremely pleased with it.

The fabric was a soft lavender silk that flattered her pale complexion. Mrs. Patel had sewn tiny beads along the scooped neck and on the bodice. It had no sleeves, but there was a draping of chiffon attached to the neckline that hung over the tops of her shoulders.

"And now, the finishing touch," declared Mirupa, as she pinned a spray of jasmine in Viola's hair.

The scent wafted in the air and mingled with the sandalwood from her bath.

"Now, if all the gentlemen do not fall in love with you at first sight, I will have not done my job properly," added Mirupa, standing back to admire her handiwork.

"Thank you. I *do* look beautiful," cried Viola, hoping that Mirupa's prediction would come true. But there was only one man she wanted to have that effect on – and would he be there?

'He is a man of his word,' thought Viola, walking downstairs, 'he will not fail to come.'

"Darling. You look wonderful!"

Aunt Mary emerged from the drawing room looking a little flustered.

"Hugo. Come and see your beautiful niece! Oh, where is he?"

"His Lordship is upstairs, my Lady," said Dinesh, who was supervising the removal of the last few pieces of furniture from the morning room where the ball was to be held.

"I said that we needed a ballroom when the house was built," complained Aunt Mary, "but did he listen to me?"

"It will be fine, Aunt Mary. You haven't invited too many guests, have you?"

"Enough to worry that there will not be enough room for all them to dance."

Just then, the Viennese ensemble arrived to add to the chaos.

Very soon the guests began to arrive. Viola eagerly scanned their faces as they entered and took their glasses of champagne, but the Earl was not among the first group, as she had expected.

By eight o'clock she was becoming increasingly agitated.

Lady Armitage and the odious Millicent had arrived and were holding court in the drawing room. Millicent was wearing so many jewels that she looked positively laden down and Viola thought the effect rather common as befitted a dancer or an actress rather than a member of the aristocracy.

At a little after eight o'clock, Dinesh announced that dinner was served.

Viola had a dreadful sinking feeling that perhaps the Earl had been prevented from coming by another uprising.

'But surely, Uncle Hugo would have heard about it?' she told herself, as she went into dinner accompanied by a colleague of her uncle.

"I've placed you between Sir Roland Martin and Mrs. Milburn. She is a dear thing and her husband has not been able to attend, so do keep her company," her aunt whispered into her ear as they sat down.

Viola looked up in time to see the Earl dashing into the hall. He said something to her uncle and then like lightning Millicent was by his side and almost dragged him to a seat next to her at the table.

Viola fumed inwardly. Sir Roland was proving to be as deaf as a post and rather seemed to have taken a fancy to her. Poor Mrs. Milburn could barely command his attention as he began to talk loudly and unceasingly at Viola.

'Oh, goodness,' she thought, as Sir Roland droned loudly on next to her. 'I have not managed to even speak one word to the Earl and, *look*, Millicent is doing her best to block him from my view.'

As she glanced over, she could see that Millicent was being unbelievably rude as she shielded the Earl from Viola's eye-line by placing her elbows on the table.

'She is making such a show of herself,' thought Viola, as she smiled politely at Sir Roland.

Eventually Millicent was forced to move as the fish course was placed in front of her. At last, the Earl looked over to Viola and smiled.

How her heart soared.

Viola found it difficult to eat her pomfret, as she was

too full of emotion to swallow the delicate fish.

"Far too many bones, if you ask me," shouted Sir Roland, as he put down his knife and fork noisily.

Viola looked up to find the Earl staring at her. She coloured and lowered her eyes.

"That Millicent is making an utter exhibition of herself," whispered Mrs. Milburn, during a rare lull in Sir Roland's monologue, "she does not seem to realise that Lord Devonport is obviously only tolerating her."

"She is very well connected and I would think that he would not wish to offend her aunt, Lady Armitage," replied Viola.

"Oh, that awful old woman," hissed Mrs. Milburn. "She is abominably rude and carries on as if she ruled the whole of India!"

Viola could not help but smile to herself – had not her aunt said just the same? "Lady Armitage is a very powerful woman," added Viola, "well, socially, at least. I gather that one's standing in Mandavi is very much judged by whether or not she approves of you."

Mrs. Milburn sniffed,

"Sadly you are correct, Miss Brookfield."

"Please, call me Viola,"

"I would be delighted. As I was saying, Viola, life here in Mandavi very much revolves around her Ladyship. She has her sights trained on the Earl as a suitable match for her niece, but I think she has some serious work to do first."

Viola felt strangely lifted by her brief conversation with Henrietta Milburn. So it *was* common knowledge that Millicent was attempting to ensnare the Earl?

'There is surely no swifter way of repelling a man than by making him feel that he is the quarry?' decided Viola.

She became distracted as the talk inevitably turned to the Russians.

"Well, I say we should just go into Afghanistan and blast the blighters. They'd soon go running off with their tails between their legs!" blustered Sir Roland.

"Hear, hear," agreed another.

"If only it were that simple," said the Earl, quietly but firmly, "but it is not just a question of chasing them over the frontier. They have been laying claim to the Northern Territories for many years and they are most persistent. Russia is a huge country with far more resources than ours."

"Sir, that is a darned unpatriotic view, if you ask me," huffed Sir Roland, whose hearing suddenly seemed to become miraculously sharp.

"The fact is, Sir Roland, that Russia has vast armies compared with the British in India. If wars are won on manpower alone, it makes our job a lot more difficult."

Sir Roland roared on and each time the Earl gave him a calm considered reply.

'He is so intelligent and wise for his years,' marvelled Viola, who could not take her eyes off him. He was wearing his dress uniform and looked even more handsome than ever.

As the port and cigars were produced, the ladies left for the morning room where the Viennese ensemble were playing jolly tunes from Gilbert and Sullivan.

"How this reminds me of England," enthused Aunt Mary, "it is many years since I was at the D'Oyley Carte, but this is just like being there."

Viola noticed that Millicent was hanging around the entrance to the room.

'Ready to pounce on the Earl as soon as he appears, no doubt!'

So far, the evening had been rather a disappointment.

She had not exchanged a single word with the Earl and it would seem that she had made such an effort with her appearance for nothing.

"Ah, here are the men," said Aunt Mary, asking the ensemble to play a waltz.

'I shall not make an exhibition of myself,' vowed Viola. 'I shall sit here and wait for the Earl to come over. Surely he will request a dance?'

But as soon as he entered the room, Millicent appeared like a shot from a cannon and demanded that he dance with her. He made an apologetic look towards Viola and took to the floor with Millicent.

"Shameless!" commented Mrs. Milburn, who was sitting next to Viola.

Then came a deep voice behind her –

"Come, Viola, will you dance with me?"

She turned round to see her uncle standing behind her.

As they danced rather stiffly around the room, Viola tried to remain relaxed.

"You are as light on your feet as your mother," he commented, as the violins swelled, "she used to love to dance."

"Yes, I recall that she did," answered Viola, feeling uncomfortable.

"She was always the belle of the ball – just as you are tonight."

Viola remained mute.

'I must ask him about the photograph,' she thought, as they wove in and out of the dancing throng. But could she? Did she have the nerve?

The waltz was drawing to a close and Viola screwed up her courage.

'I must ask him, *I must,*' she murmured, steeling herself.

Finally, as the last notes died away, she began,

"Uncle, I found a photograph of Mama the other day in a cupboard in my room. I assume that it was put there by mistake or had been forgotten about?"

She looked up at him and his face was a mask.

"Excuse me," he said quietly without responding to her question.

Viola watched as he walked away and she resolved not to let the matter drop.

'I think the only person who will give me the answer I seek is my aunt,' she thought, unaware that the Earl had left the dance floor and was standing by her side.

"So deep in thought?" he said suddenly making her jump.

"Oh, I am so sorry. I was thinking about something," she answered quickly.

"As long as it is not a *someone* you are thinking about, then I am pleased. Now will you make me very happy indeed and dance with me? I fear that Miss Armitage is set on monopolising me and that will never do."

Viola laughed and allowed him to lead her into the middle of the room. As he took her in his arms, she felt as if she had found the safe and warm place she had always dreamed about.

They whirled around the dance floor and she thought she was touching Heaven, so happy was she.

'Could this be love?' she asked herself, as she felt the strength of the Earl as he led her into another waltz.

She gazed into his eyes and sought some kind of confirmation that he felt the same way, but how would she know? She was so innocent and inexperienced in love that she did not know how to tell if a man was in love.

The Earl did not allow her to leave his side for the rest of the evening and, as he left – one of the last to depart – he asked if he might call upon her the next day.

Viola floated back to her room walking on air.

As she undressed, she noticed that the cupboard door was slightly ajar.

'Mirupa must have put the boxes from my new dresses inside.'

She pulled the door open and yes, there were the empty boxes. Mirupa had pushed the photograph to one side.

Picking it up and kissing it, Viola became determined that she would ask her aunt about it the very next day.

*

In contrast to the previous morning, the day after the ball dawned over an eerily quiet house.

Viola rose at ten o'clock and with a rapidly beating heart made up her mind to tackle her aunt over breakfast.

She quickly washed and dressed and made her way to the dining room.

"I noticed that the Earl made a great deal of fuss over you, Viola," said her aunt, mischievously, "will we be having the pleasure of his company very soon?"

"Yes, aunt, he said he would call this afternoon," replied Viola.

"How very exciting."

"Aunt, there is something I wish to ask you," began Viola, feeling anxious.

"What is it, my dear? Do you wish to ask some advice?"

"No, not really. I am hoping that you may be able to solve a mystery for me."

Aunt Mary put down her toast and gave Viola her full attention.

"It is just that I found a photograph of Mama stuffed at the back of an empty cupboard, which seems rather curious. Do you know why it is there? Perhaps I could take it out and keep it in my room?"

To Viola's shock, her aunt threw down her napkin and began to shout.

"No! No. You must not. That photo – that blessed photo – is it always to haunt me? I do not wish to speak of the thing for it is a bitter reminder that I am and always have been second best. You must forget you saw it. Promise me."

With that, she got up and ran from the room. Viola sat in her chair for a while before leaving the room.

'I must be calm,' she told herself, as she walked out onto the veranda. 'But I did not expect such a reaction. *Second best*,' she repeated to herself, as if suddenly struck by lightning. 'Mama and Uncle Hugo? No. It cannot be.'

Tears filling her eyes, Viola ran outside. Without thinking, she headed for the stables.

As she approached, Markyate was leading Snowball out to the paddock.

"Markyate! Markyate. Saddle her up at once – I am going out."

She said it with such fierceness that Markyate did not hesitate or question her.

Five minutes later she was mounted on Snowball and riding like fury out of the grounds.

'Mama and Uncle Hugo,' she wept, her tears blinding the way. 'I have to get away and make some sense of this discovery. It is too much. *Too much!*'

Urging the mare onwards, very soon she was out of sight of the house, an angry blur of black against the white coat of Snowball.

CHAPTER SIX

Viola rode until she reached the coast. Very soon, she found herself riding along the very same bay where the Earl had taken her, the day of their trip together.

She tethered Snowball to a tree as she was in need of a rest. She had ridden her hard all the way and now the sun was climbing higher.

"Poor girl," sighed Viola, as she patted Snowball's muscular neck. "You had just come back from an errand, only to be dragged out again."

Viola needed to think and the sea made her feel calmer.

'*Mama and Uncle Hugo!*' she repeated, almost unable to believe what she had discovered. 'Why have I not heard about this before? I cannot blame Aunt Mary for thinking that he only married her to be near Mama – the poor woman! I would not care one bit for being second best, but how can it still be with Mama dead? I wonder what else is waiting to leap out at me from the shadows?'

The discovery had shaken Viola terribly. Although it did not in any way diminish her mother in her eyes, it certainly made her feel differently about her uncle.

'That would explain why he has been so odd around me. When I remind him of Mama, it reminds him of feelings that he would rather forget.'

'Does my uncle love my Aunt Mary at all?' she

wondered, 'or is she living a lie? It does not bear thinking about.'

The morning was exceptionally warm and as Viola stood by the beach, the sun was so strong that she could not see across the bay. The water was as bright as a mirror and dazzled her.

She shielded her eyes and looked out to sea. It was calm and blue, much bluer than at the Isle of Wight.

Her attention was suddenly drawn off to her left where the shoreline curved round beneath the cliffs.

'I thought I saw movement,' she murmured, as she squinted hard to see. 'Perhaps it is some fishermen.'

But the figures she could make out picking their way down the beach did not look Indian. As far as she could tell, they were wearing western clothes.

They appeared to be making for a small rowing boat at the edge of the water that bobbed with the heave of the waves.

'One of them is carrying something.'

Viola was intrigued. Although she knew that she should ride straight back to the house, she was far too curious to ignore the two figures on the beach.

Presently they jumped into the boat and rowed off.

'They seem to be heading out into the Gulf,' she muttered, as the boat rounded the headland and disappeared. 'I must go and see where they came from.'

Taking off her boots, she hitched up her skirt and began to walk quickly to where she had first seen the men. The sand was damp and they had left tracks.

She followed the tracks with her eye and saw that they led to the cliffs and into a cave, which was small and hidden from the beach by a large rock. The footprints curved around it and disappeared into the mouth of the cave.

'Aunt Mary would be furious if she knew what I was doing, but I have to find out what those men were up to. They might be spies and Russian ones at that.'

There were rock pools at the base of the cliff and she dragged the hem of her skirt through the water.

Her heart was in her mouth as she approached the cave. There were strange marks in the sand nearby.

'It looks as if something has been dragged here. Goodness, I hope it's not a body!'

Screwing up her courage, Viola slowly approached the entrance to the cave.

Her eyes soon adjusted to the dimness inside.

'What is that over there?'

Viola could see something at the back of the cave that appeared to be covered with a tarpaulin.

She crept up to it and pulled it back as best as she could. It was wet and covered with sand that hurt her fingers and made her lose her grip.

At last she pulled back enough to make out a wooden hull.

'Oh, my, it's a boat. And identical to the one I just saw those men in.'

Along one side of the boat was some script in a language she did not understand. At first, she thought it might be Hindi, but the writing was too square and ugly.

'How strange – ' she murmured, fingering the letters, her heart beating fast. 'Could it be Russian?'

She fumbled her way along the boat and felt inside it. As she reached the hull, her hand touched something hard and oblong. Grabbing the end, she pulled it into what little light there was and nearly dropped it.

'It's a dispatch box like Uncle Hugo's and what is this?'

The Royal crest was clearly visible on the side of the box.

'I must go at once to Uncle Hugo and the Earl and let them know what I have found,' she said to herself, hastily putting the box back into the boat.

Just as she did, she heard a noise behind her like rustling. Eyes wide with fear, Viola spun round, but there was nothing there.

Nevertheless, her nerve had deserted her. Replacing the tarpaulin, Viola fled from the cave. She did not stop to look behind her until she reached the top of the beach where Snowball was contentedly nibbling at the grass.

"Come on, girl. Ride like the wind. We have to go and find Uncle Hugo and the Earl."

Viola had almost forgotten the reason why she had run away from the house as she urged Snowball into a gallop. All she could think of was the strange boat!

*

Arriving back at the house, Viola was almost dropping from heat and thirst. She left Snowball in the stable yard and ran towards the house. As she neared the kitchen door, she could see Anjali scrubbing pots in the sun.

"Anjali! Anjali. Is the Master at home?"

"I do not know, *memsahib*, I have not left the kitchen all morning."

Viola rushed into the cool of the house and called out to her aunt and uncle, but no one answered.

She was just deciding what to do when she met one of the servants.

"My uncle, is he at home?"

"No, *memsahib*. He left some time ago to go to Chindee. Look, he did not even have time to attend to his boxes this morning."

The servant indicated the pile of red boxes that stood in the hallway.

Viola gasped. They were the same as the one she had seen in the cave. There could be no doubt now that there was foul play going on.

"Tell me, what is in those boxes?" she asked, as casually as she could.

"It is very top secret, *memsahib*. But they are from the Viceroy in Calcutta."

"Goodness. It is even more important than I thought,' she said to herself, as she ran into the dining room and poured herself a glass of water.

'I cannot wait for Uncle Hugo to return. I must go to the Earl at once. I think I can remember where he said his office is – he described the market nearby – it should not be too difficult to find.'

Viola pulled hard on the bell and waited for Dinesh.

"Yes, *memsahib*?" he said, as he calmly appeared in the doorway.

"Would you order the buggy ready for me at once, please?"

"The buggy, *memsahib*?"

"Yes, Dinesh. And at once, please."

"Very well, *memsahib*, if you insist. Will I ask someone to accompany you?"

"No, I will go on my own. Now hurry!"

Viola ran upstairs and quickly changed her dress and grabbed a hat. She did not want the Earl to see her looking less than her best.

By the time she returned downstairs, the buggy was outside the front porch.

'There is no reason to sit and wait for Uncle Hugo – this will not wait,' she told herself, as she cracked the reins over the head of the chestnut horse.

She found the market quite easily and next door stood some tall Government buildings. Viola paid a boy a couple of rupees to mind the buggy and rushed inside.

A uniformed official intercepted her as she ran though the revolving doors.

"Can I help you, miss?"

"I am looking for Lord Devonport, it is urgent that I see him."

"I am afraid that he is having luncheon, miss, but he is due to return shortly. Would you care to wait?"

Viola sighed but took the wooden chair that the official was offering her.

'I cannot imagine that half an hour will make any difference, so I will have to be patient.'

She sat there for fifteen minutes and as the moments ticked by, she began to think that, perhaps, she was being very silly about the entire matter.

'Perhaps there is a perfectly innocent explanation and I am fretting unnecessarily,' she told herself. 'I am probably imagining a lot of nonsense about Russians after Aunt Mary's hysterical chatter. After all, it may not be Russian on the side of the boat.'

She was on the point of leaving, having convinced herself that she was indeed overreacting, when on the dot of two o'clock, the door swung open.

Viola looked up and saw the Earl with Millicent hanging smugly onto his arm.

"Viola! What a lovely surprise," he said, smiling charmingly at her, "to what do I owe this pleasure?"

For a second Viola was tempted to walk away, but there was something in Millicent's over-pleased expression that awoke a new determination inside her.

"I have come to see you about something I wish to bring to your immediate attention," she said, hoping that he would take the hint and dismiss Millicent.

"Then you must come into my office at once," he replied.

To Viola's dismay, far from leaving them to speak alone, Millicent grasped the Earl's arm tighter and did not budge an inch.

'Oh, that girl is just too much,' thought Viola, 'if I were her, I would gracefully retire.'

But Viola realised that Millicent viewed her as competition for the Earl's attention and so would not be easy to remove.

'Perhaps I should insist I see him alone – ' she thought as the three of them walked upstairs to his office.

But again doubts were creeping into her mind as to the veracity of what she had seen. She knew that most men disliked anything they would consider 'women's hysteria' and she now felt foolish for acting on impulse.

"I suppose you have been invited to the Duke of Morpeth's ball this weekend?" asked Millicent as they reached the Earl's office, obviously confident that Viola had not.

"I could not say for certain," replied Viola, mortified, "my aunt was rather preoccupied at breakfast this morning and she did not mention it."

A look of pure triumph crossed Millicent's face. She curled her lip and stared down her nose at Viola as the Earl opened his office door and held it open for them.

"Oh, I think it is certain that Lord and Lady Wakefield will have been invited, Miss Armitage," said the Earl, neatly puncturing the balloon of Millicent's pride. "Besides, the invitations have only just been issued and it was only because your aunt called on the Duchess the previous evening that you had yours before anyone else."

"Nevertheless, you must promise me the first dance," pouted Millicent, preening her tight curls and rolling her eyes in a way that Viola thought was most unladylike.

The Earl simply smiled politely in reply,

"Perhaps some tea, ladies?"

Viola nodded her head and wished that Millicent would disappear into thin air.

But instead, she flounced over to a Georgian chair with an upholstered silk seat and sank down into it, rearranging her skirt as if settling in for a long stay.

"Now, what was this matter you wished to discuss?" began the Earl.

"Perhaps later – " answered Viola, hoping that after finishing their tea, Millicent would take her leave.

There was an awkward silence while they waited for the tea to arrive, punctuated only by the Earl's observation that the weather was rather stuffy.

Millicent sat and glared at Viola, not moving an inch.

"Ah, here is our tea," declared the Earl, as a tray was brought in.

'I can tell that he is feeling uneasy in this situation,' thought Viola, 'so why does he not ask her to allow us to be alone? Surely he is only being polite to her?'

"My uncle was called away to another disturbance early this morning," said Viola, thinking that if she bored Millicent with politics, it might do the trick.

The Earl looked concerned. His brow furrowed and he put down his teacup in a resigned manner.

"This is most unfortunate – do you know where it was?"

"My aunt did not say but uncle left very early indeed. I did not hear him go."

"It is becoming a most frequent occurrence," he replied, "and it is not making my work here any the easier, for each time it happens, I am called away from my task in hand to help out."

"Are you not, as part of the Army, engaged to take care of such insurrections?" asked Millicent.

"My primary function is not to quell riots," answered the Earl, a little tersely, "although I am forbidden from disclosing the nature of my task, suffice to say that I do not welcome these unfortunate distractions."

Viola decided that she must take the bull by the horns and request a moment alone with the Earl, but just as she was about to speak, there came a knock at the door.

"Yes, Simpkins, what is it?"

"Y-your next appointment is here, my Lord," he stammered.

"Ladies, I am sorry to have to dismiss you after such a pleasant intercourse, but I will have to take my leave. The gentleman who has come to see me is an important official from London and it would not do to keep him waiting."

Millicent threw the Earl a petulant glance and cocked her head on one side like a sulky child.

"So soon? Oh, Charles. I suppose I am now going to have to make do with the first *two* dances at the ball?"

"We shall see, Miss Armitage, now would you ladies excuse me? Thank you so much, Miss Brookfield, for coming to inform me of the latest disturbance, once I have finished here, I shall go to Lord Wakefield's office to discover more."

'Oh, Heavens! He thinks I came here to tell him about my uncle,' thought Viola, as the Earl showed them to the door. 'Bother Miss Millicent Armitage!'

As they walked in silence towards the exit, Viola's mind was whirling.

'I am such a fool for not insisting that I see him alone and now it is too late. He believes that I came on an altogether different errand.'

She was still thinking hard as she thanked the boy for minding her buggy.

'If I return to the cave and take one of the boxes as evidence, he could not dismiss my theory as the ramblings of an overheated imagination. If it *is* Russian, then he will know, and if it isn't, I shall replace the box at once.'

Viola urged the horse on as she debated if she should drive straight to the beach.

But what if the strange men were lurking nearby?

'Perhaps I could persuade Markyate to accompany me – I do not fancy going back there alone and defenceless.'

Even though Viola could be impulsive, she usually tempered it with good, solid common sense. Had not her Mama always told her to think hard before acting?

'I cannot go to my uncle and discuss it with him – how can I look him in the eye until I have made some sense of this situation with him and Mama?' she reasoned, as she drove the buggy home.

Pulling up outside the house, Viola felt nervous at seeing her aunt after leaving her in such emotional turmoil.

'I shall take my lead from Aunt Mary,' resolved Viola, as one of the boys ran to take the reins from her. 'If she does not mention this morning, neither shall I.'

"Darling! There you are."

Aunt Mary came towards her as she entered the hall. There were no signs that she had been distressed and Viola was pleased that she seemed to have recovered.

"Where have you been? It has been so hectic here. So many comings and goings. First, an invitation has arrived for a very smart soiree next week and then there was the messenger from Bombay – "

"I went for a ride in the buggy and then called on Lord Devonport's office."

"You have been gone for so long that I was worried about you. I was about to send Markyate out to find you."

"I can look after myself, aunt."

"That may well be, but I am not happy for you to be out alone. The messenger brought news that a platoon of Russians have been sighted close to the Afghan mountains and with this disturbance in Chindee – "

"Has Uncle Hugo returned, then?" asked Viola.

"No, not yet – " she replied, looking a little uncomfortable. "Actually, I have a confession to make. I am afraid I was a bit naughty and read the messenger's letter."

Viola was quite horrified.

"Aunt. Uncle would be most unhappy at you reading his private correspondence!"

"What he does not know will not hurt him. Besides, if he refuses to tell me anything, how do I know what is going on? However, this latest news does mean that we should make ourselves ready to pull out of Mandavi – if the Russians are so close, I would not feel safe here."

"Will uncle agree to leave?" asked Viola, panicking that she might have to leave the Earl behind and that he would then fall straight into Millicent's clutches.

"He would be reluctant to make such a decision, but I might insist that you and I are sent to Bombay until things are under control. I do not fancy being murdered in my bed by a Russian spy. They say they are all over these parts."

"But surely, we are safe here? We have the servants to look after us."

"They would be no defence against the Russians. The main reason I worry so is that your uncle will insist upon bringing those blessed dispatch boxes home."

She pointed to the pile in the hallway.

"So many secrets," continued her aunt, "and they make us a very vulnerable target for kidnappers and murderers. I have told him countless times that I do not wish to have them in the house, but he does not listen to me."

Viola stared at the red leather boxes – they seemed to throb in front of her. Yes, she was now certain that she had seen one of them in that cave.

"Where is the uprising that uncle has gone to?"

"Oh, somewhere near the Chitterdee Road," answered her aunt vaguely.

"Goodness! I rode past there this morning. I did not see any disturbance."

Aunt Mary shot her look of pure horror.

"Please, tell me that you were not there on your own?"

"Why? I know the way – the Earl took me riding there recently to show me the Duke of Morpeth's home on the cliffs."

Aunt Mary advanced towards her and grabbed her shoulders. Her fingers dug hard into her flesh as she shook Viola.

"You must never, never go there again on your own. *I forbid it*!"

"But aunt – "

"No arguments, Viola, it is a dangerous place even when there are no riots. What foolishness is this? A young English girl riding out alone and defenceless at a time when the natives are already angry? Do I have to spell out to you what could happen? You must not go out unaccompanied again, ever. Do I make myself clear?"

Tears sprang into Viola's eyes. How could she go back

to the cave now that her aunt had expressly forbidden her to go there?

"I am very sorry, aunt, I promise I will not go out again on my own."

Aunt Mary let go of Viola's shoulders and seemed satisfied.

"Good, I am glad to hear it. Now, I have instructed Mirupa to pack you an emergency bag, so go and check that she has done it properly."

"When will we leave?"

"I have not decided yet, but it could be at quite short notice. I will wait to discuss the matter with your uncle when he returns later."

Tearfully, Viola made her way up to her bedroom. She looked through the small case that Mirupa had just finished packing and then dismissed the girl.

'I *cannot* leave now. There is too much at stake,' she sobbed as soon as Mirupa had closed the door. 'Not only that, but if we go, it will mean not seeing the Earl again. I cannot let him fall into Millicent's waiting arms – *I love him*!'

Falling to her knees, Viola prayed for all she was worth. She asked God and she even implored her parents in Heaven to intervene.

'Please, let us stay in Mandavi,' she cried, tears soaking her dress. 'Mama. Papa. I love him. I cannot go now – I would rather stay here and risk death itself. *Please*, help me. I beg of you.'

CHAPTER SEVEN

Lord Wakefield did not return to the house that evening. Aunt Mary was beside herself with worry as she paced up and down the drawing room after dinner.

Viola sat and read while her aunt tried to distract herself. But as ten o'clock struck and Viola said that she was ready for bed, Aunt Mary became more agitated.

"I shall not sleep until Hugo is back," she howled, wringing her hands.

"Please, aunt, you must rest. If anything has happened to him, we would have been notified by now," said Viola, trying to soothe her.

Even though she pretended to read, Viola's mind had been working hard to find a way to slip out of the house and back down to the beach. She even wondered if she could persuade Markyate to accompany her, but she concluded that he was too loyal to the Wakefields and that her entreaties would fall on deaf ears.

Eventually a messenger on horseback arrived at the house. Aunt Mary nearly fainted when he came striding into the hall covered in dust.

But he was merely carrying a note telling her that Uncle Hugo had been delayed at Bhuj.

"Bhuj! But that is so far North. What is he doing there?"

"I am sorry, Lady Wakefield, but I cannot divulge that information. Rest assured that he is well and the fighting has subsided."

"Well," she exclaimed, as the messenger was shown out. "Why on earth is he in Bhuj? It simply does not make any sense."

"At least we know he is safe," said Viola, "now it is late and we should retire."

"This wretched business. It makes me want to leave for Bombay at once."

"But aunt, we do not know that this has anything to do with the Russians. Let me ring for Dinesh to bring you some brandy."

"Thank you. I do not know what I would have done had you not been here with me. This is not the first time Hugo has been away overnight and I do worry so."

Viola made her aunt comfortable on the sofa and rang for Dinesh. He soon came and returned with a glass of brandy.

"Drink this, Aunt Mary, it will help you sleep."

"Sleep. I could not think of it. You go on up to bed and leave me. I shall sit and wait for your uncle. I do not sleep much these days anyway. It is the curse of being old."

Viola laughed softly and kissed her aunt goodnight.

She too could not sleep and lay awake for hours. But it was not thoughts of her uncle that kept her awake, but of the Earl and the prospect of leaving Mandavi.

*

Viola was woken early the next morning by raised voices on the landing. She could tell by her uncle's deep boom that he had returned and it appeared that he was having an argument with Aunt Mary.

Viola tiptoed to the door and listened.

"But we have to leave. It is not safe," she heard her aunt screaming.

"Out of the question, Mary. If we go, what will it do to the morale of everyone who depends upon us? Those who look up to us? People will panic. No, we are staying and that is my final word on the subject."

"If we are all murdered in our beds, it will be forever on your conscience."

Viola could hear the tear-soaked voice and her heart soared out to her, but at the same time, she was relieved that they would now not be leaving Mandavi.

'Thank you, Mama. Thank you, Papa,' she whispered.

For she truly felt as if her parents had gazed down from Heaven and had extended a helping hand.

She walked quietly back to bed and lay down.

When she did finally arise and make her way down for breakfast, she could sense that there was something of an atmosphere in the room.

Her uncle was at the table, reading his newspaper, while Aunt Mary silently ate her toast.

"Viola, how are you?" she cried, upon seeing her niece enter the room.

"I am quite well, thank you, and I am glad to see that you have returned safe and sound, Uncle Hugo."

He looked up from his newspaper and nodded.

"It was quite a difficult situation."

Viola waited for him to elaborate further, but he simply resumed reading.

"Hugo, I have asked Viola not to go riding on her own any more because of the current crisis. I hope that you are in agreement with me?"

"Absolutely. Viola would be most unwise to do so. It does not do to go flaunting oneself in front of the locals. You are in my charge and I am afraid that I must insist on you staying put until the current problems have abated."

"You cannot mean – "

"I do. You must stay confined to the house for the time being. A round-the-clock guard is being posted at the entrance and neither you nor your aunt should go out unless accompanied by Markyate."

'Confined to the house,' thought Viola, 'so I shall not be able to slip away to the cave. I will need to think of an excuse, but how I will do that, I do *not* know.'

She finished her breakfast in silence.

'What will I do all day long? I will die of boredom.'

Viola hoped that perhaps the Earl would ride over and pay her a call, but with all this unrest she thought it most unlikely that he would have the time to spare.

'Really, I did not anticipate when I came to India I would end up becoming a virtual prisoner. I would be better off on the Isle of Wight!'

Yet deep down she knew that had she stayed in England, the lingering sorrow over the deaths of her parents would have engulfed and overtaken her.

'And I would not have met the Earl,' she reminded herself.

"I hope that you will be able to amuse yourself this morning," said Aunt Mary, interrupting her thoughts. "I have a number of letters to write and then I must supervise the gardeners as we are planting some new trees."

"Very well, aunt," replied Viola, resigned to a morning of tedium.

"There is always your uncle's library, if you are bored. He has a fine collection of literature that he brought with him from England. I do not know if you read French or German, but I believe there are some interesting works there."

"I am afraid that my French leaves a lot to be desired," Viola replied, "and I do not speak a word of German. Languages were never my forte. I preferred composition and needlework in the classroom, and horse-riding out of it."

"Ah, yes, I remember your Mama telling me what a fine horsewoman you were becoming and it is a pity that you will have to curtail your excursions on horseback for the time being. That is, unless the Earl pays us a visit."

Her aunt eyed her expectantly, as she had sensed that something had occurred when Viola had visited him in his office, but Viola had yet to tell her about Millicent.

"I think the Earl is rather busy at present," answered Viola, somewhat distractedly. "I do not believe we shall see him whilst the current situation lasts."

"Tell me, dearest, did something happen when you went to see him? You seem somewhat sad when you speak about him."

"It is Millicent Armitage."

"I see. She has her cap set at him, has she not?"

"She has. And what is more, she is most forceful in making her intentions clear. So unladylike. I know I did not have an appointment to see the Earl, but he had said that I would always be welcome. But when I arrived, there was Millicent clinging onto his arm as if she had been sewn to it!"

"Shameful behaviour. I would have thought that Lady Armitage would have something to say, but perhaps she has her aunt's blessing."

"What do you mean, Aunt Mary?"

"Perhaps she has it in mind to make a match between them. The Earl is quite a catch after all and very handsome."

"Would she really countenance such shocking forwardness in order to achieve the desired outcome?"

"I think the question is more if the Earl would fall for such an obvious approach," answered her aunt. "I would hope that he is not the sort to be dazzled by the prospect of an entry into such an important family. He has his own considerable fortune, a title and houses here and in England and he seems intelligent and kind."

"All admirable virtues, but men can be swayed by beauty and Millicent is very pretty."

"Darling, have you not looked in the mirror recently?" she said laughing, "you are a most beautiful young woman. Far more attractive than Millicent and furthermore, you are well brought-up, intelligent and thoughtful. For all her money, she dresses like an actress and behaves commonly."

"Aunt," said Viola, quite shocked. "That is a terrible thing to say about her."

"It is true nevertheless and I hope that she behaves herself at the Duke's ball this weekend."

Viola's eyes lit up.

"Have we been invited?" she asked, eagerly.

"Yes, we have. Oh, do forgive me, dearest, yesterday was such an awful day that it went right out of my head. You will enjoy visiting his house – it is quite the most wonderful place and it sits right on top of cliffs overlooking the bay."

She rose from the table, leaving Viola to ponder what she had said. But her mind was racing at this latest turn of events. They had been invited to the ball at the Duke's house after all!

'Perhaps it will afford me the opportunity to return to the cave? There must be a way. If we are going to his house for the ball, could I not just slip away and take another peep at that boat to see if the boxes are still there?'

The more she thought about it, the more it became apparent that this was the only way forward.

Viola toyed with her napkin as she reflected on the earlier part of the conversation. Her aunt was definitely encouraging her not to lose hope that the Earl might be attracted to her.

'Does Aunt Mary really think that the Earl could prefer me over Millicent? Has she seen something in his demeanour that would lead her to believe that there may be a chance for me?'

At last, Viola rose and wandered towards the library. She had not seen it since her aunt first showed her around. But now, housebound, she found herself looking forward to exploring it.

The walls were covered with books from floor to ceiling and there was a set of wooden library steps resting against the wall.

'It does not appear that this room is used very often and it strikes me that it has an unused air about it. I suppose uncle is too busy to spend much time reading.'

She scanned the shelves, searching for something that might interest her.

Viola wondered if her uncle might have some books written in the strange alphabet that she had seen in the cave, but she could not see anything likely.

Climbing up the library steps, she found a section full of French novels. Some were in French and some in English. Her eyes rested on a row of novels by Balzac.

'Ah, I can remember Papa reading and enjoying this author,' she reminisced, scanning the titles, *Cousin Bette, Eugenie Grandet, Old Goriot –* '

She pulled a volume of the latter out and looked at the cover.

'This was one of Papa's favourites. I shall choose this one.'

As she started to climb down, her foot slipped and she dropped the book. As it flew through the air, a piece of paper fluttered out from between its pages.

'What on earth could that be?' she thought, righting herself on the steps and carefully descending. She retrieved the book that had landed on its side and bent for the paper.

'It is a letter,' she murmured, picking it up.

But as she looked at the writing, her heart lurched.

'It is Mama's handwriting!'

Just at that same moment, there was knock on the door and Dinesh entered. Hastily, she tucked the letter into the waistband of her skirt.

"Oh, Dinesh," she gasped, still reeling from shock.

"Lady Wakefield is out on the veranda and wishes to see you."

"Right away," she answered, and followed him out of the door.

'Why was a letter from Mama hidden in the book?'

Her aunt was sitting composing a letter while keeping an eye on the gardener who was digging a hole for the sapling that lay on the path beside him.

"You wanted to see me, Aunt Mary?"

"Yes, dear. I am writing to my Solicitor in London as I want to change my will. I wish to leave everything to you on the event of my death."

"Oh, aunt, let us not speak of death. You have years in front of you yet."

"Nevertheless, I wanted to tell you that you and your children will benefit."

"Aunt Mary, I do not wish to sound ungrateful, but I am already quite wealthy due to Mama and Papa's deaths."

"Yes, I know. But your uncle and I were not blessed

with children of our own and so I want you to have everything. I do not wish there to be any undignified wrangling. Some of our cousins will inevitably be up in arms about it, but there it is – I have made my decision."

"So, you believe that I will have children, aunt?" Viola asked shyly.

"Naturally."

"I am not certain that I will ever marry, Aunt Mary."

"You must not be defeated, darling. If you love the Earl, as I believe you do, then you must not let a silly girl like Millicent spoil your dreams."

Viola looked at her aunt, shocked at her words.

"Is it really that obvious that I am in love with him?"

Aunt Mary patted her niece's hand and smiled indulgently.

"My dear, if I was your age, I should be in love with him too. I have seen the way he looks at you and I have no doubt that he returns your feelings."

"But he has not declared himself to me and he allowed Millicent to drag him off to luncheon."

"He is a polite man and I am certain that he did not spend luncheon praising her beauty. He is aware that her aunt is a very powerful force in Mandavi and that many doors would close if he was seen to be aloof or offhand with her. No, until Millicent throws herself at him and he has to reject her, he knows he cannot cause offence by making assumptions as to her intentions."

Viola heaved a sigh of relief. It was so good to be able to talk to another woman. It was at times like this when she missed her mother. She had been able to talk to her about anything and she would always come up with just the right advice.

Aunt Mary, it would seem, was cast from the same mould.

"Thank you so much," she said gratefully and walked out into the garden with her book. "You have set my mind at rest."

*

The hot sun and a delicious lunch made Viola feel somewhat drowsy, so she decided to go upstairs to her room for an afternoon nap.

When she opened the door, Mirupa was sponging down her lilac ball gown.

"*Memsahib* – you startled me," she exclaimed, dropping her sponge.

"I am sorry, Mirupa, but I am rather sleepy and would like a nap."

"Then you must let me help you out of your clothes. Will you be wanting to wear your lilac at the ball you are going to this weekend?"

Viola looked at the dress and sighed. The Earl had already seen her in it once and she wished she could wear something else.

"As we are not allowed out of the house," she grumbled. "I will not be able to go to Mrs. Patel's and get something else made in time."

"Do you not have a dress that I could perhaps remodel for you?"

"You, Mirupa?"

"I may not be as accomplished as Mrs. Patel, but my embroidery is much admired. See, I made this scarf myself."

Mirupa handed her the end of her scarf. It was covered in the most exquisite beading and embroidery.

"It is beautiful. Do you really think you could do something with one of my dresses? I did bring a black ball gown with long sleeves, but it is quite plain.

"If you could show me which one it is, I can see what I could do."

Viola went over to the wardrobe and rummaged around inside and pulled out her black satin dress. Mirupa examined it closely, nodding her head while she turned the seams inside out and plucked at the neckline.

"I think I can do something with this, if you will permit me. Would *memsahib* prefer shorter sleeves?"

"I do believe I should prefer no sleeves at all," answered Viola.

"Then I shall do my best. Let me take it away and I will have it ready for you by Saturday morning. Now, come here and allow me to unlace your bodice."

Viola let her untie the laces and relaxed as the bodice fell open. Mirupa was just undoing her skirt when something fell to the floor.

"Oh, what is that?" she asked.

Viola suddenly remembered – it was the letter!

"Thank you. I had quite forgotten that I had put it there."

With the black dress over her arm, she closed the curtains and left Viola alone.

Quickly, she unfolded the letter and began to read,

"My dearest Hugo,

I felt I had to write to you after your sudden departure yesterday evening. I am aware that my rejection of your marriage proposal has hurt you deeply and I am sorry to have caused you sorrow. You are and always will be a dear, dear friend but I am afraid that my feelings are no more than that of friendship. I regret that I cannot accept but, as you know, I am already in love with Jonathan Brookfield and have every intention of accepting him as and when he proposes. I wish you well and hope that in time we can resume our friendship.

Yours, Alice."

Viola almost dropped the letter.

'So this explains so much of what has happened. Uncle Hugo proposed to Mama before Aunt Mary and was obviously very much in love with her. No wonder Aunt Mary believes that she is second best. Uncle Hugo must have gone on to court her shortly afterwards, as it is dated June and Mama and Papa married in November.'

She lay down on the bed and thought for a long time about the letter.

'What a strange place to hide it. Poor Uncle Hugo. It certainly explains why he has been so odd with me. As so many remark, I do look like Mama when she was young."

Viola had gained a new understanding of her uncle and she felt less uncomfortable with him as a result.

'And he must have found some happiness with Aunt Mary – they were always laughing together when I was small.'

She eventually drifted off to sleep, feeling considerably happier.

*

She had not been asleep for long, when Mirupa came in and woke her up.

"*Memsahib*. I am so sorry to wake you but there is a young lady to see you and she is most insistent that she see you urgently."

"Who is it, Mirupa?"

She handed Viola the card that the visitor had given her.

"Miss Millicent Armitage," read Viola. "Oh, thank you, Mirupa. Let me dress and I will be down presently."

Viola found a clean dress and put it on quickly.

'What on earth can she want?' she thought.

By the time that she had gone downstairs, curiosity had been replaced by the certainty that the unheralded arrival of Millicent had something to do with the Earl.

Viola composed herself as she entered the drawing room. Millicent was standing by the window wearing blue silk that did not suit her in the least.

"Millicent," began Viola, coolly, "to what do I owe this pleasure?"

Millicent spun round and threw Viola a challenging look.

"I will get straight to the point, Viola. I thought it was time that you and I had a woman-to-woman chat."

"Then, please be seated."

She sat down and immediately began to speak,

"It is obvious that we both have feelings for Charles," she said, baldly, "and I am here to tell you that as I saw him first, I believe I have rights over him. I have come to ask you to withdraw gracefully, while it is not a competition exactly – how could it be? Nevertheless, I want you to leave the way clear for *me*."

Viola was almost speechless at Millicent's audacity. She sat for a moment before replying. All the while, Millicent's eyes burned with a fervour that was quite unnerving to behold.

"I do not know what to say – " said Viola, after a while.

"There is nothing to say, Viola, your quest is hopeless. He will never love you – an orphan with no status in the world, living off the charity of her family."

A surge of hot anger rose up in Viola. Who on earth did this girl think she was, coming into her home and ordering her around? She bit her lip and tried to remain calm. At last, she answered,

"Millicent. Far from living off the charity of relatives, I am very wealthy in my own right and secondly, I have no intention of *withdrawing gracefully* as you put it. It is up to the Earl to choose to whom he pays court and if he seeks my company, then I shall not rebuff him."

Millicent turned pink and then red, a slow flush spreading up from her neck and over her cheeks. She stood up, clutching her small silk bag so tightly that Viola thought she would pull the handle clean off.

"Is that your last word on the subject?" she fumed.

"*It is.*"

"Then I will do everything in my power to make certain that the Earl is made aware of the kind of woman you are and that he should have nothing, I repeat, *nothing* to do with you."

Viola stared at her. Millicent had issued a challenge and she was not about to back down.

"As you wish. Now, please leave."

Viola moved to ring for Dinesh, but Millicent was already heading for the door, her face crimson with rage.

She swept out of the room, almost knocking Aunt Mary clean off her feet.

"Goodness! Was that Millicent Armitage?" she puffed, taken aback, "she did not even stop to say hello or goodbye."

Viola sank back down on the sofa and sighed.

"Yes, it was and I am afraid that she has thrown down the gauntlet."

"What on earth do you mean?"

"She came here, aunt, to tell me to 'withdraw gracefully'."

Aunt Mary gave her a puzzled look and then

realisation dawned on her.

"Ah, the Earl?" she asked, in a low voice.

"Yes."

"Then you have just made a powerful enemy indeed, Viola. If she came out of her way to speak to you directly, she will stop at nothing to make a match with him. Dearest, the path of true love will not run smoothly if Millicent has her way."

Viola rose and walked to the window. The furious form of Millicent could be seen stomping her way along the drive. Even at that distance, Viola could see her burning hatred and furious determination.

"Could she really ruin my prospects with the Earl?" she wondered, suddenly feeling not so brave, now that Millicent had left.

Doubts and uncertainties were crowding her mind as she knew that her aunt was right. Millicent was a force to be reckoned with in Mandavi and she had a most powerful woman behind her.

"Darling, do not fret. What is done is done and you were right to send her packing. All is not lost."

'But is it?' thought Viola, her heart sinking.

She wanted the Earl more than anything in the world and now it appeared that she would have to fight for him.

'I cannot let Millicent succeed. I can't and I won't!'

But deep down inside, she was not so confident.

She stayed watching the disappearing figure of Millicent until she could no longer see her. Suddenly, the prospect of the Duke of Morpeth's ball took on an altogether different aspect.

'I shall not give up on him until he tells me to go away and leave him alone,' she resolved whilst hoping fervently that it would never come to pass.

CHAPTER EIGHT

But it was not long before Millicent started wreaking her revenge.

The next morning, Viola and Aunt Mary were sitting on the veranda when a letter was delivered to the house.

"Oh dear," muttered Aunt Mary, reading the note. "It seems as if Millicent has been pouring poison in her aunt's ear already."

"Why, what does the letter say?"

"It is from Lady Armitage. I was supposed to be going to see her this afternoon for tea, but she has cancelled and without giving an explanation."

"And you think that Millicent might be responsible?"

"Darling, you are without a malicious bone in your body and it would not occur to you to do anything so mean, but the same cannot be said for Millicent."

"Oh, Aunt Mary, I am so sorry. This is my fault. Lady Armitage is one of your old friends and now, because of me, she has withdrawn her friendship."

"Do not concern yourself, Viola. I want you to concentrate on making yourself as attractive as possible for this Saturday's ball. Millicent will not spare any expense on her gown, while you will be having to make do with the same lilac dress you wore at our party."

Viola smiled and put down her book in triumph.

"But you are mistaken, aunt, I shall wear a new dress for the ball. Well, a new *old* one."

"I do not understand – " began her aunt, clearly puzzled.

"According to Mirupa, she is rather good with a needle and has offered to remodel a black silk dress I brought with me."

"That is wonderful. Darling, you are very clever."

"It is not I who is clever, but Mirupa. She is a highly resourceful girl."

"Yes, I know, which is why I wanted her to look after you. She has always been one of my best servants. She comes from a very good family, you know."

"I believe she did say something to that effect. So, it rather makes one wonder why she is working as a servant?"

"Her family have fallen on hard times and there are many mouths to feed. It is the usual story in these parts. The people are still very poor and you may not realise it yet, Viola, but there is a huge disparity in India between the rich and the poor."

Viola was just about to answer when Dinesh brought in another letter.

"Yet another missive from the Armitages, perhaps?" suggested Aunt Mary.

She looked at the letter and paused.

"Oh, this is not for me, darling, it is for you."

She passed it over to Viola, who looked more than a little surprised.

She took the note and stared at the writing.

"I do not recognise the hand – "

Viola's hand was trembling as she pulled open the seal.

What she read inside made her heart sing with joy.

"It's from the Earl," she cried, "and he says that he is sorry he has not been able to pay us a visit, but his work leaves him no time to do so."

Viola paused as she read the remainder of the letter.

"And furthermore, he asks that I will reserve the first dance for him at the Duke of Morpeth's ball. And to think that I believed it was from Millicent."

"You see, I told you not to concern yourself unduly," replied her aunt, a huge smile on her face. "Millicent means nothing to Charles."

"He may have written this before she came to see me."

"No, I think not."

"Then we need to celebrate!"

"I will ring for some *nimbu pani*," Aunt Mary proposed.

Viola wanted to sing and dance. She stood on the veranda and swayed in time to the music in her head – the same waltz she had danced to with the Earl.

'I have won the first round against Millicent,' she thought, triumphantly. 'In spite of what she may believe, she cannot yet influence the Earl against me.'

She was still waltzing when Dinesh brought in the *nimbu pani*.

*

The rest of the week passed in a haze. It remained extremely hot and Viola did little except walk around the garden and sit by the fountain.

She kept rereading her Mama's letter. She debated whether or not to ask her aunt about it, but after her reaction to the photograph, she thought it best not to.

The day of the ball soon arrived and she was almost

too excited to eat. After breakfast, Mirupa brought her a parcel.

"Is this my dress?" she asked, excitedly. "I can hardly bear to open it."

"Please, *memsahib*, you must. I want you to try it on to see if it fits."

Viola held her breath as she undid the string and pulled open the wrapping.

"Mirupa. This is so gorgeous!"

Mirupa had reworked the bodice and sewn on hundreds of jet beads. The sleeves had been taken out and the straps narrowed and covered with black chiffon.

"I have also taken the liberty of making you this as you admired mine so much," she said, offering her a matching wrap made of black silk chiffon so fine that it was almost transparent. At each end, hundreds of silver and black beads sparkled.

Viola took it and hugged Mirupa.

"Thank you. Thank you so much," she cried, tears springing to her eyes.

"I want you to be the most beautiful lady present," said Mirupa.

"In this dress, I shall be. Oh, I cannot wait to put it on."

"Then, why not try it now?"

Viola ran upstairs and quickly began to undress.

The dress felt as light as air as Mirupa helped her into it and it fitted perfectly.

"Am I correct in thinking that you have taken the waist in a little?" she asked.

"Yes. You have such a tiny one it seems a shame not to show it off."

Viola blushed. She was not used to servants making such personal comments, but then again, she had learned quickly that Mirupa was no ordinary servant.

Looking in the mirror she was delighted with her reflection. The dress suited her fair skin perfectly and it made her look so elegant and feminine.

"Every man will definitely fall in love with you," repeated Mirupa.

"There is only one man I wish to look on me with love," murmured Viola, still secretly thrilling to the unexpected surprise of the Earl's letter.

"I have brought you some special bath oil and I shall go into the garden just before you leave and find some flowers for your hair," added Mirupa.

Viola felt confident that she would be most attractive lady at the party. Millicent, although pretty, always had a somewhat sulky look about her.

'And not all men care for such curly hair – ' she thought.

But in spite of her excitement, Viola was reminded by the black dress that she was still in mourning for her parents.

'How I wish that Mama and Papa could see me now,' she thought, a little tearfully. 'I look so like Mama in this dress that even I can see the resemblance.'

She wondered what Uncle Hugo would do when he saw her.

'Perhaps I will broach the subject with him and say I have found the letter.' But she then discounted the idea immediately. What if her aunt did not know of its existence?

Viola doubted that she did, as it looked as if it had been hidden away for many years. She did not wish to cause her upset as inevitably it would.

At last, it was time for her to get ready. Mirupa drew

her bath with great ceremony and threw flowers into the hot water before she poured in the scented oil.

After the bath, Mirupa brushed Viola's thick blonde hair a hundred times until it shone and arranged it into an elegant style. She topped it off with a large exotic flower with a wonderful scent.

Next it was time to put on the dress.

Finally Viola was ready. She draped the wrap around her shoulders and as she moved towards the door, she could smell the sandalwood and jasmine from her bath and the perfume of the flower in her hair.

She felt exotic and ravishing.

As she descended the stairs, she whispered to herself,

'This could be the most important night of my life'

She went into the drawing room where Aunt Mary was waiting for her. Both she and Uncle Hugo gasped out loud as Viola entered the room.

"Darling. You look so beautiful," Aunt Mary greeted her, almost crying as she rushed to kiss her.

"I agree, Mary, Viola does us proud," commented Uncle Hugo, a little stiffly.

Viola noticed that he swiftly looked away again.

'He does not wish to be reminded,' she thought to herself.

The carriage was ready and waiting and soon they were on their way. Aunt Mary chatted as they drove along, but Viola's mind was firmly elsewhere.

She had decided to try and slip away from the party and explore the cave, even if it meant leaving the Earl in the ballroom at the mercy of Millicent.

'I feel certain that she means nothing to him now that he has written to me,' she thought, nervously. *'Now, all I have to do is make him fall in love with me.'*

The carriage arrived at the Duke's house and as she was helped out of the carriage, she noticed a small path that appeared to lead off down to the cliffs.

"Excuse me, but where does that path lead to?" she asked a footman.

"It goes down to the beach, miss," he replied, "but you are not advised to go there after dark."

Viola simply smiled. She had every intention of doing just that!

She suddenly felt shaky. Not only was she about to see the Earl and Millicent, but there was the question of when she could slip away on her secret mission.

There was usually a break in the dancing halfway through the evening, she remembered, to allow the orchestra to rest. Could she possibly make her escape then?

'And there is the problem of Millicent – she will be watching my every move like a hawk,' she said to herself, as they walked up to the front door. 'Oh, I do hope she is not going to cause a scene tonight. I know that she will not give up her chance to monopolise the Earl without a fight.'

Viola grew nervous. Millicent was a formidable foe and what if she had turned the whole of Mandavi against her? Perhaps nobody would speak to her –

'And if I do manage to escape, will the boat still be in the cave? I shall feel so stupid, as well as cross, if I waste precious dancing time and then it has gone.'

Thinking that she was full of trepidation simply because of the Earl, her aunt took her arm as they entered the ballroom.

"No need to be worried, darling," she whispered, "you are the most beautiful girl in the room. See how all the gentlemen are admiring you?"

She soon spotted the Earl in a corner of the room. He

was chatting to a group of Officers in uniform.

He turned to see her and immediately his face lit up. He quickly excused himself from his comrades and came rushing over.

"Miss Brookfield, might I say how lovely you look this evening?"

"Thank you so much and you must call me Viola. I think we are now sufficiently acquainted with each other to dispense with the formalities."

"Then I insist that you call me Charles," he answered, smiling so that his green eyes crinkled at the corners. "Did you receive my note?"

He gave her such a beseeching look that she realised that he too was nervous.

"Yes, I did and I would be delighted to take the first dance with you."

The Earl grasped her hand and kissed it, all the while looking into her eyes.

"Then I shall see you when the music begins," he said, in a low voice that made her quiver in anticipation.

Viola's head was reeling as he walked across the room. Aunt Mary squeezed her arm excitedly.

"He certainly seemed very pleased to see you. And look, Millicent witnessed the entire scene."

Viola looked up in time to see Millicent, standing with Lady Armitage and a group of other elderly women – a look of pure fury upon her face.

"Did Lady Armitage acknowledge you?" asked Viola, still feeling guilty.

Aunt Mary looked so sad when she admitted,

"No, she has not."

"I am so sorry, this is all my fault."

"Darling, I have already told you, it is that horrid Millicent who is to blame. Do not worry. Lady Armitage and I have fallen out before and still we live to fight another day!"

She was trying to be gay, but Viola saw that she had been deeply hurt by Lady Armitage's snub.

Viola and her aunt stayed on the fringes of the dance floor waiting for the music to begin. They talked very little and Viola felt as if all eyes were upon her.

"They say that the Russians have been sighted in the Gulf of Kutch!" said her uncle, who had suddenly appeared behind them.

Both Viola and Aunt Mary jumped as he spoke.

"Goodness, Hugo. Must you creep up on us like that? And who is talking such nonsense?"

Viola listened without comment, but her heart was beating so hard that she felt certain that her aunt and uncle must hear it.

'Russians in the Gulf,' she thought. 'Now there can be no doubt as to who owns that boat.'

"Sir Khengarji, the Ruler of Kutch. The top man himself, Mary. He is furious that secrets are being passed to them and I'm dashed if I know how. It appears that dispatch boxes are going missing and before you alarm yourself, they are disappearing *after* they have left our house."

'It is a Russian boat for certain,' thought Viola, wondering if she should tell her uncle about her discovery.

She was still pondering the issue when the orchestra began to tune up.

'Perhaps I should tell Uncle Hugo. After all, it might not be safe for me to go alone. But if I do tell him, he will take every last man in the place with him and I shall forfeit my dances with the Earl.'

And so Viola decided that she would slip away on her own.

"You are certain that these boxes are disappearing *after* they have left the house, Hugo?" asked her aunt, suspiciously, "because if I find out that Russians are sneaking into our home and running around, I will be on the next train to Bombay."

"Do not alarm yourself, Mary," he replied, "you are quite safe."

Viola felt sick with nerves as she looked up to see the Earl marching towards her. He had barely reached her when, out of nowhere, Millicent appeared with a sulky look on her face.

"Charles, you promised you would dance this one with me," she pleaded in a wheedling tone of voice whilst twirling a curl around her finger.

"I am sorry, Miss Armitage, but you must be mistaken. I have already promised Miss Brookfield the first dance. Viola?" he added, offering her his arm.

Viola felt as if it was a dream as he led her onto the dance floor. Immediately, his strong arms took her in his charge as they swept around in an elegant waltz.

"I confess that I have never seen anyone more lovely than you are tonight," he whispered, as the *Blue Danube* swelled in her ears. "You are so very beautiful. I am breathless with admiration."

Viola lowered her eyes as her heart sang. She moved nearer to him as they danced and it thrilled her to be so close.

'I love him so much,' she thought, as she gazed up into his warm green eyes, 'would it be too much to hope that he might care for me?'

As they swung round, she caught sight of Millicent who was dancing with an elderly gentleman. She shot Viola a look full of vitriol.

Viola tried not to take any notice, but Millicent's glares followed her everywhere.

'I feel so safe in his arms,' she told herself. 'That Millicent cannot possibly hurt me or take away this wonderful feeling.'

The Earl continued to dance with Viola for hours. She barely realised how time was slipping away until the orchestra stopped playing for a short intermission.

It was growing hotter in the ballroom and it occurred to Viola that her aunt and uncle were nowhere to be seen.

Much as she was loath to leave the Earl, she knew that she had to seize the moment and creep down to the beach.

"Please excuse me, I shall not be long. I must find my aunt," she said, as the Earl once again kissed her hand.

"I shall be here, waiting," he murmured with a meaningful look.

Hurrying away, Viola felt as if a part of her was being torn in two – so reluctant was she to leave his side.

'But I have to do it. I shall run down to the beach, find out if the boat is still there, grab a box and then return to the ball.'

Going out into the garden, Viola noticed that there were torches stuck into the earth. They were just the right size for her to carry, so when no one was looking, she selected one that was nearest to the path to the beach and hurried away with it.

The path was quite steep and terribly dark and almost as soon as Viola had left the garden, she began to feel afraid.

Her slippers slid on the dusty path and there were strange noises in the bushes.

Screwing up her courage, she ran as fast as she was able and soon, she found herself on the beach.

The moon was rising in the sky and sent beams of

silvery light across the bay. Viola scanned the dark horizon for signs of ships, but could see nothing.

The sound of her heart pounding seemed louder than the gentle surge of the waves over the shore and she hoped that her torch would not alert any Russians.

'I must go inside. *I must*,' she urged herself, standing at the mouth of the cave.

It seemed far deeper and darker than it had during the daytime and it smelled strongly of seaweed.

Taking a deep breath, she felt her way into the cave, holding the torch aloft.

'It all looks so different at night,' she said as she strained her ears for any signs of the Russians.

The torch lit up the inside of the cave and Viola was relieved to see that the boat was still where she had last seen it.

'It does not appear to have been moved,' she observed.

She noticed too that the tide had been in, as the sand on the floor no longer bore the marks of where the boat had been dragged inside.

She crept forward slowly holding her breath in fear.

At last she stretched out her hand to grasp the tarpaulin.

It was wet and slippery and try as she might, she could not pull it back with just one hand.

'Oh, bother,' she hissed, sticking the end of the torch into the wet sand so that she could use both her hands.

In the flickering light, she could see that her slippers were ruined and that the hem of her dress was covered in wet sand and seaweed.

She tutted loudly, but resolved to carry on. Grabbing the tarpaulin with both hands, she pulled at it until it slid off the boat.

'Thank Heavens,' she cried, as she saw that there in the base of the boat was a red box. 'All has not been lost.'

She leaned over and picked up the box. It felt heavy yet curiously dry.

'Is this the same one I saw the other day?' she wondered. 'It is difficult to tell as they all look the same. I do not know how uncle can tell them apart.'

She slid her fingers under the flap and it popped open.

Viola gulped as she saw that it was full of documents.

And on the very top was a slip of paper with writing on it. She screwed up her eyes and tried to read it.

'This is from one of Uncle Hugo's staff.'

But try as she might, she could not read the signature.

'Now, if only I could see more – "

But terrified of setting her dress alight, she gave up.

'I will have to read it when I return to the house and now I shall hurry back to the ball before I am missed.'

Tucking the box under one arm, she bent down to pick up the torch. She turned round and to her utter horror found herself staring right into the face of a man!

She realised with a sinking heart that he could only be Russian.

He snatched the box from her and immediately another man grabbed her wrist so hard that she felt it would break.

The taller of the two said something in a strange language and put the box under his arm.

"What have we here?" he said in heavily accented English.

The man who had hold of her wrist, twisted her arm behind her back while the other snatched the torch from her.

Without realising what was happening, Viola found

her hands tied tightly with some rough rope that bit into her slender wrists.

Everything moved so quickly that she felt as if she had entered some terrifying nightmare.

"Please, let me go," she pleaded.

But the man with the torch simply barked something to his companion, who then dragged Viola out of the cave and onto the beach.

"Let me go!" she shouted loudly, hoping that someone might hear.

But even as she did so, she realised that the music up on the cliff tops was loud enough to drown out every last sound.

She soon found herself being dragged down the beach, while the two Russians conversed in staccato tones.

'I am being abducted,' she deduced, as they pulled her towards a waiting boat that bobbed on the waves. 'I must leave a clue for the Earl to find – my slippers!"

Almost as soon as she had the idea, she let one ruined slipper fall off her foot and into the sand. She prayed that the Russians would be too intent on dragging her into the boat to notice.

They picked her up as if she was a puff of air and threw her into the boat and jumped in after her with the box.

"Where are you taking me?" she screamed. "I demand to know!"

The men simply laughed at her and began to row off into the bay.

"You keep quiet or I make you quiet," said one of them.

Viola noticed that it was he who seemed to do most of the talking. She assumed that the smaller Russian did not speak English, as he remained grimly silent as the boat pulled away from the shore.

Viola fell mute. She had quickly guessed that if she made a noise, she would come to harm. She looked at the two men. They were roughly dressed and wore fierce expressions. Judging by their manner, she supposed that they had made this trip on many an occasion as they wore an air of quiet confidence.

'Where are they taking me?' she thought miserably as they passed the cliff.

She looked up and heard the faint strains of music drifting on the night air.

It was colder now that they had left the beach and she shivered.

One of the Russians roughly threw what appeared to be a sack at her. It scratched her skin and gave little protection from the sharp wind.

Tears began to well up in her eyes.

'I must not cry. I must not,' she told herself, as the wind whipped at her hair. The flower that had looked so exotic earlier fell crushed and broken into her lap. It made Viola want to weep and she felt as if her courage was fast deserting her.

'Perhaps the Russians will kill me or even worse – ' she ruminated, grimly, as they rowed on into the black night. 'Will the Earl come and find me or am I doomed to die? Oh, Charles. I have never needed you more than I do now. Do not let me down. Find a way to bring me back safely.'

But that thought made her cry unashamedly, as she shivered in the boat.

Would she see the next day? Or was this where her Indian adventure ended?

She prayed with all her might that the Earl would somehow find her.

CHAPTER NINE

Viola did her best not to show how terrified she was. The small rowing boat was pitching and tossing as they progressed towards the open sea.

'Where can they be taking me?" she wondered, lowering her head so that her captors could not see that she was silently crying. 'Surely they cannot be taking me all the way to Arabia in a rowing boat?'

The Russians remained silent and Viola was beginning to wish that she had eaten more at the ball.

'But I was so preoccupied with the Earl, and keeping an eye on Millicent's movements, that I only ate the merest morsel. And now, here I am, kidnapped. Are they going to kill me? Or harm me in some other way?'

She looked up to see on the horizon a ship coming towards them. It was all lit up and its funnels belched thick white smoke.

'That must be theirs,' she thought, as the two men became more animated.

Very soon, they drew along side and a rope ladder was thrown down.

'Heavens. I shall never make it to the top in this dress,' she thought, fearful of what they would do next.

But as the rope ladder tumbled into the boat, so too did a winch with a seat.

The larger Russian grabbed her arm, untied her hands and dragged her to it.

"Sit," he commanded.

Viola knew that to resist would be foolish, so she climbed into the seat. She was past caring what she looked like, which was just as well as the lower portion of her dress had soaked up bilge from the boat and was ruined.

The seat swung perilously as it was heaved up and over the side of the ship.

Numerous hands pulled her from the winch and roughly threw her to the deck.

Viola hurt her bare foot as she landed and it was bleeding.

An older man, who looked as if he might be the Captain, barked an order and soon a sailor appeared with a torn piece of sheet. He bound her wound and Viola stared in horror at the dirty cloth that sufficed as a bandage.

'I shall die of a terrible infection,' she moaned. 'Oh, I do hope the Earl finds my slipper and comes after me. The ship must still be in sight of the shore.'

But would he guess where she was?

The Russians were now talking loudly amongst themselves and it sounded to Viola as if they were arguing about her.

"What do you want from me?" cried Viola, in a weak and tired voice.

But the men ignored her plaintive cry.

Instead, she was bundled along the deck and forced down steps that led below. It was dark and smelled of oil and a whole host of other unpleasant odours that made Viola catch her breath and feel ill.

The corridor was narrow and dimly lit and the man behind her kept prodding her hard. They seemed to walk on and on, down and down, until at last, they reached a door with a grille at eye level with all the bolts on the outside.

The man grunted and pushed her inside. Viola flew in through the door and on to the floor. As she was picking herself up, she heard the door being bolted.

She looked around the room. It was bare save for a wooden pallet at one end that she supposed served as bed.

'Perhaps they are going to hold me to ransom,' she wondered, as her eyes became accustomed to the dim light. 'Or maybe they think I know secrets and they will torture me. Oh, I wish I had not gone down to the cave. I should have told the Earl about my discovery, rather than be too clever. I should have trusted that he would believe me without having to wave a dispatch box in his face.'

But Viola knew it was too late. She was imprisoned on a Russian ship and her future was uncertain.

'What if we are bound for Russia?' she thought with a sinking heart.

She remembered that the Gulf of Kutch was opposite Arabia and that beyond lay Afghanistan, Turkistan and then *Russia*.

'I cannot live through such a long sea journey,' she wept, 'especially if I am cooped up in this dreadful cell.'

*

Meanwhile, back at the ball, the orchestra had resumed playing.

The Earl searched for Viola but could not see her anywhere.

"Are you not going to ask me to dance?" demanded Millicent, who had taken full advantage of Viola's absence and had run straight to the Earl's side.

"Of course," agreed the Earl, his eyes still straying around the room as he offered her his arm. As they danced, his thoughts strayed constantly to Viola – his heart calling silently to hers.

*

Back on the ship, Viola did not see a soul for an hour or so. There was a tiny porthole at the top of the wall, but it was still so dark that no light came in save for when the moon appeared from behind a cloud.

Her mind was whirling.

'As they have not killed me at once, perhaps I am of some use to them alive. Why would they want me? It has to be something to do with the dispatch boxes.'

Viola felt so frightened that she got down on her knees and began to pray.

'Please, Lord, deliver me from this ghastly place. Do not let me die. Please help me."

Next she prayed that her Mama and Papa would, in some way, deliver their beloved daughter from her perilous situation.

Viola prayed as she had never prayed. She urged God with all her might to help her. She prayed until her knees hurt and her voice grew hoarse with pleading.

'The Russians are very clever enemies,' she thought, as she forced herself to lie on the hard wooden pallet. 'They know that they will not encounter any resistance in Afghanistan, and are now waiting until India shows signs of weakness before they pounce. And what is in Uncle Hugo's dispatch boxes will help them to find out what our Army is planning.'

The gravity of her position began to sink home.

'Either I shall be killed or forced to be a traitor to my country,' she realised, 'they cannot know that I am the niece of one of the most powerful men in India, so they have taken me as hostage to help them decipher the documents.'

Viola knew that many of them would be in code which she could not read.

'Oh, this is a hopeless. I can only hope and pray that the Earl gathers a search party to find me and that this ship does not set out to sea again.'

It was true – the ship had not moved an inch since she had boarded it. Not long after she had been flung into the cell, she had heard the grating sound of the anchor being dropped and now the ship bobbed gently on the waves.

The relative calm was suddenly shattered when she heard a commotion of voices outside her door and the sound of the bolts being scraped back.

'I must be brave, whatever happens,' she resolved as she stood up.

"You come with me!"

It was the Russian who had abducted her. He stood at the front of a group of frightening looking men, who stared at her with thinly veiled contempt.

As one of them grabbed her tied hands, she yelped with pain. The ropes had been on for so long that they had bitten into her wrists and made them bleed.

They forced her to walk along a corridor and up some stairs. Very soon she found herself in a room that was furnished with a table and chairs.

"Sit," the Russian ordered, as he pulled out a chair.

"My name is Sergei and you will help us."

"I do not see how" she began, her heart sinking as her fears were confirmed.

"You will read these out to us."

He gestured to a pile of dispatch boxes that one of the sailors had just brought in and put on the table.

"I speak English, but none of us reads your language. We find the letters too difficult and so unlike ours."

"Never," cried Viola, her eyes shining with defiance. "I must have food, I must have water."

Sergei said something to one of the sailors who picked up a jug of water. Viola's mouth was so dry that seeing the water was like torture.

With a cruel laugh the man threw the water in her face.

The others all laughed loudly too, much to Viola's humiliation. The water dripped down her face and she was so desperate that she let it trickle into her mouth.

Sergei loomed up in front of her again.

"You will read it in English and I will translate. That is an order. You do this or you will get no food or water ."

"I – will – never – comply," replied Viola as she tried to regain her dignity.

Sergei rattled off something in Russian and Viola was then dragged to her feet again and out of the cabin.

In no time at all, she was back in her cell and the door was bolted behind her.

Viola burst into tears. Her hair hung in a soggy mess around her face and she felt utterly defeated. Her foot was now throbbing where she had been dragged through the corridors and the bandage was hanging off.

'I am so exhausted,' she sobbed.

After a while, she lay down on the hard bed and tiredness took over. She eventually fell into a deep sleep, trying to stay warm by wrapping her skirt round her.

*

"Have you seen Viola?"

Aunt Mary was fast becoming alarmed. She had been looking for her niece for the best part of an hour and it seemed that she had disappeared into thin air.

Lord Wakefield was chatting to some elderly men in the corner.

"Hugo, Viola has gone missing!"

He looked irritated and attempted to dismiss his wife.

"Don't be foolish, Mary, she is probably out in the gardens."

"But I have looked in the gardens and she is not there. Neither is she in the conservatory nor anywhere in the house."

"Then she has returned home."

"The carriage is still outside where we left it."

"Then maybe someone else gave her a lift in theirs. Look, Mary, if it makes you feel better, I will go home and see if she is there."

He turned to his friends and bade them goodnight.

"If she is not at home," he muttered as he climbed into their carriage, "I shall return within the hour."

But he did indeed return an hour later and his face was as white as a sheet.

"She is not at home," was all he said.

Aunt Mary let out a wail that could be heard throughout the house. The music stopped and the Earl came running over as she fell into a swoon.

"Lady Wakefield, whatever can be the matter?"

"It is Viola," she cried. "I knew she was too headstrong for her own good and now she is probably lying dead somewhere!"

"Please, tell me what has happened," asked the Earl, in a calm voice.

"I don't know why you are so worried, she probably just went for a walk," came Millicent's annoyed voice.

The Earl spun round with his eyes full of fury.

"Miss Armitage. This is not the English countryside and Miss Brookfield has not just gone for a breath of air or to pick strawberries! We are in India and it is a dangerous place for unaccompanied young ladies. Viola's life could be in peril. Now do you see why I am so concerned?"

Millicent's mouth fell – she stared at the Earl in disbelief.

"Well," she pouted, "all this fuss about a silly orphan who cannot do as she is told!"

The Earl's face throbbed with fury. He grasped Millicent by the arm and led her towards the hallway.

"Miss Armitage, Viola is twice the person you are. If you cannot hold your vicious tongue and help us look for her, I suggest that you leave at once."

Millicent looked as if the Earl had slapped her – she had such a shocked look on her face. She turned around on her heels and flounced out of the room. The Earl watched her exit with contempt in his eyes and returned to Lady Wakefield.

"Do you think that Viola is in danger?" she asked, her voice quivering.

The Earl gave a grave reply,

"If she was foolish enough to go to outside the grounds on her own, who knows what harm she might have come to? Lord Wakefield, we must form a search party at once. I suggest that we arm ourselves."

Viola's uncle nodded and rushed off to gather the men together.

"Do not fret, Lady Wakefield. We shall find Viola, I promise," said the Earl.

"I blame myself. I am meant to be looking after her in this country and if I cannot even do that –" replied Aunt Mary. She was in floods of tears.

The word soon went round that Viola Brookfield had disappeared in mysterious circumstances and so the party came to an abrupt end.

A few of the women, led by the Duchess, took it upon themselves to comfort a distraught Aunt Mary, whilst the Earl and Uncle Hugo organised two search parties.

Lord Wakefield's party struck out to scour the surrounding countryside, while the Earl was just about to head off when the footman, who had spoken to Viola earlier, came forward.

"My Lord, is the young lady in question blonde and wearing a black silk dress?" he asked, a little sheepishly.

"Yes," answered the Earl, "do you know something, man? If so, tell us now."

"The lady enquired earlier about the beach path," said the footman, pointing towards it. "She asked where it led and I told her. She seemed very interested."

The Earl did not hesitate.

"Come on, men," he shouted to the assembled throng. "This way."

"They *must* find her," sobbed Aunt Mary, as she watched the line of torches bob along the path to the beach. "I shall never forgive myself if anything has happened to her."

*

Viola suddenly awoke in her cell and almost at once it hit her where she was. Her bones ached and she was terribly thirsty.

'I wonder what time it is. Oh, how I long for something to drink.'

The sky was still dark and, even though she felt as if she had been asleep for hours, she realised that she must have only dropped off for a while.

She heard a noise in the corridor outside and she looked up towards the grille.

It was Sergei.

"Ah, I see you are awake. Have you changed your mind? Will you help us? Look, I have some water for you."

He held up a jug of water so that she could see it. Viola thought quickly. She needed water desperately.

"Give me some water and I will look at the dispatch boxes," she agreed.

"Good. You have seen sense," he said, unbolting the door.

He came into the cell and untied Viola. She could smell alcohol on his breath.

'What will he do to me? I must stall for more time.'

Sergei untied her hands and led her back to the room with the dispatch boxes.

Viola sat down and waited while he undid one and took out a sheaf of papers.

He poured her a glass of water and she downed it greedily. He replenished the glass and then sat opposite to her, staring at her expectantly.

"Now the papers, please," he ordered.

Reluctantly, Viola took the sheaf he was offering her and scanned them.

'Oh, dear, they are in some kind of code that I cannot read.'

"Well?" Sergei asked.

"I would like to take some time to look at them. It is difficult to read them."

"Why can you not read them now?" he demanded with a threatening air.

"They are in a code," admitted Viola, "and I need time to translate it."

"But you will translate?" he snarled in a way that was an order more than a question.

"I-I will try," said Viola, her voice wavering.

Sergei stared at Viola but she could not determine what his thoughts might be. His face was a closed book. Finally, he spoke.

"You are very clever girl, you find our hiding place for boat," he said. "We see you first time you go there and thought you might return."

"So I did hear a noise that day. Why did you not take me prisoner then?"

"We thought you just a silly girl – now, we know who you are."

Viola was horrified. Surely they could not know?

"Then, who am I?"

Sergei laughed.

"We have spies in this part of India and they tell us all we want to know. You are daughter of important man. You worth a lot to us."

'Heavens! They think I am Uncle Hugo's daughter and not his niece,' she said to herself, stunned.

The door to the cabin opened and another man came in carrying a tray. He took off the cloth and Viola saw that it held bread and cold meat on a plate.

"Eat now and later, you read code. Dmitri will guard you, so do not think of escape."

As if to reaffirm what he said, Dmitri smacked a large wooden cosh into his hand in a threatening manner and glared at Viola.

"Now eat," ordered Sergei, getting up to leave the room.

Viola did not need to be encouraged. She fell upon the food like a ravenous wolf. The bread tasted strange and the meat was pork – not her favourite – but she ate it all the same.

"I will be back in three hours to see how you have done. Do not fail at this task or you will feel my displeasure."

'I have to think of a way of to get out of this,' she thought. 'I have no idea what I am going to tell the Russians. Surely, they will unmask me as a fraud? I can no sooner read this code than I can converse with them in Russian. Oh, where is the Earl? I do so pray that he discovers where I am and comes to find me.'

But in her heart, she thought that it would be a miracle if that happened. She ate the last of the simple meal and picked up the dispatch box with a sigh.

*

The path to the beach was very dark. The Earl marvelled at how Viola had found her way down. Not only was it steep, but the bushes were full of thorns.

'Viola, my own dear love. I am coming,' he said to himself.

He had not said anything to Aunt Mary, but he knew that Russian ships had been sighted along this coast. It was one of the reasons why he was in Mandavi after all. He hoped that his suspicions that she had been abducted were unfounded.

Presently his search party emerged onto the beach. The tide was coming in and the Earl cursed. It would soon wipe away any traces of Viola's footsteps.

"Hurry men," he called, "look along the shoreline for signs of tracks and do it quickly as the tide is against us."

The party broke up and the men combed the shoreline.

'Viola. Please hold on,' he entreated silently. He was just realising what she meant to him.

"Over here!"

A shout went up at the far end of the beach. Everyone ran forwards.

"Look, some tracks."

The Earl looked and there were the footprints of three people. Two, he judged, were men and the other one was most peculiar. There was just one footprint and one shoe print.

'She has lost a shoe,' he thought, rapidly.

No sooner had the thought struck him than another cry went up.

The man was waving an object in his hand.

"What is it?" shouted the Earl.

"A slipper, my Lord. I have found an evening slipper."

The Earl ran down the beach and took it off him. Yes, it was Viola's.

He lowered his torch and studied the maze of footprints in the sand. He could clearly see that Viola had dragged her heel in a long line that headed for the shore.

'Clever girl,' he muttered, as he began to follow the line in the sand.

It led to the shore and the Earl could see that a boat had been moored there.

"They have taken her out to sea in a rowing boat," he said in a low voice.

"What can we do, my Lord?" asked one of the party.

"Let me think for a moment – " he answered as his eyes scoured the horizon, whilst thinking, 'Viola, darling. I know you are out there somewhere.'

The Earl ordered his party to keep searching the beach for more clues. One of them offered him his pocket telescope.

"I noticed you seem to be looking out to sea, my

Lord," he said, handing him the object, "you will see better with this."

Gratefully, the Earl took the telescope and unfolded it. The night was still dark, but he knew what he was doing.

Putting it to his eye, he could see nothing but blackness. But then there was a light. He adjusted the focus and then, there were lots of lights.

"A Russian ship," he murmured under his breath.

"What can you see, my Lord?"

"It is as I feared, Albert," he said to his colleague, "she has been kidnapped by Russians. Do not alarm the rest of the men as yet, but there is a ship right out in the bay. This has happened before – when I was in Hyderabad last month, some Russians kidnapped the daughter of a high-ranking official and ransomed her in return for secret information."

"Did the young lady in question escape?"

"We never found her," the Earl replied quietly.

Albert was just about to say something when another shout came from the top of the beach under the cliffs.

"My Lord, we have found a cave and there is a boat in it. We think it's a Russian vessel."

The Earl and his colleague strode up the beach to where the others had now gathered. Two of them were dragging the boat out of the cave as he approached.

"It looks as if there was a scuffle inside," remarked one.

"What is this?" said another, picking up something black and covered in sand.

He handed it to the Earl.

His jaw worked silently as the sodden cloth unravelled in his grasp. It was Viola's chiffon wrap. The beads glittered in the light of the torches.

"It is Miss Brookfield's," he announced. "I think we

can now safely say that she has been abducted by the Russians."

There was a stunned silence as the rescue party took in what he was saying.

"Is the boat seaworthy?" he asked, after a long pause.

"I think so, my Lord," answered the man who had found it.

"Then let us drag it down to the shore. Albert and I will row out to sea. There is a Russian ship moored in the bay and I believe Miss Brookfield to be on it. You, you and you, will also come.

"The rest of you – go back to the house, find Lord and Lady Wakefield and tell them that we are still searching for Miss Brookfield. Do not, in any circumstances, let Lady Wakefield know that we believe that her niece has been taken by Russians. However, someone should take his Lordship to one side and inform him."

The men he had chosen to accompany him began to drag the boat across the beach while the others returned to the house.

The Earl could see their torches dancing along the path as they went.

Very soon the Earl and his men were rowing out over the dark ocean. He repeatedly looked through the telescope to check that they were heading in the right direction, his thoughts filled with Viola.

'I am on my way, my darling,' he said to himself. '*Be strong*, Viola, dearest, be strong. I am coming for you!'

The men rowed silently on into the black night as the Earl pleaded with God that he would find her still alive when they eventually got there –

CHAPTER TEN

The Earl urged the two rowers to make all haste as they ploughed on through the dark night. As he looked back, he could still see the lights of the Duke's house, high up on the cliff.

"There rests a very worried woman," he commented.

"Would that be Lady Wakefield, Miss Brookfield's aunt?" asked Albert.

"Yes, it is. She is the one who invited her to India. Viola's parents died recently and her mother was Lady Wakefield's sister."

"We had better find her, then, my Lord. You know how these Russkies can be dashed tricky."

"I know," he answered, grimly.

"You are thinking of that case we encountered when we first arrived in Mandavi – the diplomat's daughter?"

The Earl nodded and how he hoped, with all his heart, that history was not about to repeat itself.

'I wish I had told Viola that I love her,' he thought, as he put the telescope to his eye and watched the blinking lights of the Russian ship draw nearer. 'I had intended to make my feelings known to her this very evening at the ball. But I became a coward and too concerned that she might say she did not feel the same.'

He thought too about Millicent. Had he really been so foolish as to have been flattered a little by her flirtatious attentions?

'She will attempt to do me much harm for the way I have spoken to her tonight,' he thought and then resolved to try and smooth the situation over with her once they returned with Viola safe and sound.

*

Viola was beginning to panic on board the ship. She had searched through the dispatch box and she had found that some of the papers were not in code.

She was just about to hide them when two men came bursting into the cabin.

It was Sergei and a man who Viola thought must be the Captain.

"Three hours cannot have passed already?" said Viola, looking up.

"Captain is in a hurry. He wants information now," replied Sergei, a steely look in his eyes.

"I-I – "

The Captain glared at her and barked something to Sergei. He waved his finger right in Viola's face and picked up the papers before she had a chance to move.

"Captain say you must translate."

"But I told you before – they are in code."

Sergei scanned the papers and at once curled his lip into a snarl.

"These not code. Now read!"

Viola was shocked – how had Sergei known that the papers were not coded?

'He must be able to read some English, otherwise he could not have discovered that fact,' she thought with a rapidly sinking heart.

She wondered how she could possibly stall, but the look on the Captain's face told her that she was not going to be able to put him off for long.

"I-I cannot," she stammered.

Sergei translated for the Captain and almost immediately, his face turned red and he started shouting.

Viola could not help herself, she began to cry.

That seemed to enrage the Captain even more and he dived into his coat and pulled out a knife. Still shouting in Russian, he waved the knife around and brought it right up to Viola's cheek.

"Captain say you read or he will cut you if you do not co-operate," translated Sergei with obvious relish.

With the blade against her face, Viola had no choice.

Slowly, she began to read the document in front of her.

"Memo from Sir Richard Melding to Lord Wakefield with regards to the positioning of troops on the Gulf of Kutch," she began.

She halted while Sergei translated for the Captain. He grunted and took the knife away from her face.

"Continue," ordered Sergei.

Viola read on, but made sure to omit certain important details such as the amount of troops and where they would be stationed. There were some phrases that she did not understand as she was not accustomed to military terminology and so she omitted those as well.

But she could tell by the way that Sergei was glaring at her, that he was suspicious that she was not telling him everything.

Unfortunately so did the Captain.

In a blind fury, he began to shout at the top of his voice and raised the blade.

Viola cowered as low as she could and covered her face. She sat there, expecting to feel the sharp sting of the blade, but next she heard Sergei talking to the Captain.

Peering through her fingers she could see that the Captain was putting his knife away and had retreated from the table.

"You are not telling us all we need to know," said Sergei, calmly, "you will go back to your cabin and think about it. You get no food or water until you agree to read us everything."

Sergei pulled Viola to her feet and dragged her back to her cabin.

"You silly girl," he hissed. "You will stay here until you come to your senses."

Just then, another member of the crew appeared and began to shout a stream of Russian at Sergei.

"Da, da," he answered and quickly followed him down the corridor.

Viola, crying with relief, crept to the door of her cell and tried the handle.

'He has not locked it,' her heart leapt. '*It is open.*'

Without even pausing to think how she might escape from the ship, Viola carefully opened the door and crept outside into the corridor.

She scarcely drew breath as she moved slowly towards the stairs to the deck.

'I wonder where Sergei has gone?' she thought, as she inched her way along.

'What if he suddenly appears? Will he harm me?'

Viola realised that Sergei had a terrible temper and might well prove to be violent. She knew little about Russians but supposed, judging by comments at the ball that evening that they were easily roused.

'Shall I ever see the Earl again? Or Aunt Mary?' she mumbled, as she mounted the stairs.

*

Meanwhile, unbeknown to Viola, the little rowing boat with the Earl and his men on board had drawn up alongside the Russian ship.

"One of you must stay with the boat," whispered the Earl, as Albert skilfully threw the grappling hook they had found in the boat up over the side of the ship.

Albert tugged on the rope to ensure that it had a firm hold before signalling to the Earl that all was well.

"You go first, my Lord."

The Earl deftly scaled the rope and was soon heaving himself over the side.

It was quiet on deck as he jumped down. Immediately, he crouched low and waited for his comrades to join him.

He noticed that the man who stood watch on the bridge was snoring over the wheel, his black cap falling over his eyes as he slept.

The Earl signalled for the men to split up and go in different directions, but each was clear as to their purpose – to find Viola Brookfield.

*

Viola reached the top of the stairs with bated breath. The door was heavy and she was afraid that it would make a loud noise if she tried to open it.

'There is bound to be someone watching,' she thought, debating whether or not to attempt to turn the brass handle. 'And where will I go once I am on deck?'

She realised that her escape plan was somewhat ill thought out. She supposed that there might be a rowing boat alongside the ship.

'But I have never so much as picked up an oar in my life,' she told herself with a sinking heart, 'and how will I make it down to where it is moored?'

Finally she screwed up her courage and pushed the brass handle down. With an immense effort, she managed to open the door.

Outside, it was dark save for a few lanterns around the deck. She could hear the slap-slap of the waves against the ship and the cold wind whipped through her.

'It is now or never,' she decided, and hurtled forth – *straight into the Earl*!

"*You*," she cried, as the Earl clapped his hand over her mouth.

"Ssh," he urged, his eyes sweeping the decks, "do not make a sound. I will get you off this ship."

Tears sprang into Viola's eyes as he put his arms around her.

"I thought that I would never see you again," she murmured, as his strong arms enfolded her.

"Darling Viola. I would have died on the edge of a Russian blade before that happened, for *I love you*. I love you with all my heart and it took you being in peril of your life for me to tell you."

Viola looked up at him with wide eyes. Could she really be hearing this? Was she dreaming?

"*Charles*," was all she could say, as their lips met in a warm and loving kiss.

Viola felt the deck spin away from her feet and her heart leap for joy. *The Earl loved her and she loved him*!

"Darling," he muttered, not letting her free from his embrace for a moment, "we must make haste. There is a rowing boat moored alongside the ship and one of my men is waiting. Do you think that you can make it down the rope?"

Viola was trembling all over. She had never known such joy – such ecstasy. She gazed into his green eyes and felt as if she could drown in them.

"I will – try," she answered at last.

"Then, hurry. There is no time to lose."

A low whistle alerted the Earl to the presence of his men and quickly they regrouped and ran to where the waiting boat was bobbing below.

"Do not be afraid. We must move before they realise that you have escaped," said the Earl softly as he held Viola's hand and gazed into her eyes.

But Viola was terribly afraid as she inched her way down the rope.

'I must not look down. I must get to the boat,' she told herself, as she was helped down by the Earl.

She was very relieved when she finally reached the rowing boat. She collapsed into a heap as soon as her feet touched the ground.

Within seconds, the Earl was embracing her, a concerned look on his handsome features.

"Darling, are you all right?"

Viola nodded weakly.

It was not long before the other men had climbed down the rope and joined them. Albert took up the oars with another fellow and they began to row as fast as they could away from the Russian ship.

"They tried to make me read them the secret documents," wept Viola, who was suddenly overcome with tiredness and emotion. "That day I came to your office when you were having luncheon with Millicent – I came to tell you that I had discovered a strange rowing boat hidden in a cave and that I had found dispatch boxes concealed in it. But you were so occupied and I did not like to trouble you. I thought that if I brought you a dispatch box, you would believe me."

"Did you not think I would have acted on your word alone?" asked the Earl. Viola hung her head. She felt rather silly now.

"You were very foolish and very brave," continued the Earl, tenderly, "and you have been lucky to escape with no more than a few cuts and bruises. These men are brutes and they could have done far worse to you."

"Dearest Charles, if only I had not been so headstrong. But I felt that I had to bring you firm evidence. Uncle Hugo was not at home when I returned and so, when we received the invitation to the Duke's house, I resolved to slip away and find the boxes. I believed that all I had to do was to take one and return to the ball. I did not think for an instant that I would be captured."

"We now know it was some locals who were in league with the Russians who have been stealing the dispatch boxes," explained the Earl. "Our intelligence has confirmed it in the last few days. Viola, *I* would have believed you – no matter how wild your claims. You must know that I love you deeply and trust you implicitly?"

Viola sighed.

The Earl held her close and she felt as if she was indeed safe at last. So safe, that she soon fell asleep in his arms lulled by the gentle sound of the waves as they headed in towards the shore.

It seemed as if everyone from the ball was standing with torches on the beach waiting for the Earl's return. Aunt Mary was right at the front of the crowd, being comforted by the Duchess.

A cheer went up as the little rowing boat came into view.

"Is my niece in the boat?" beseeched Aunt Mary, as she wrung her hands together. "I cannot see well at the best of times and it is so very dark – "

"Yes, I can see her," answered the Duchess with joy. "And everyone appears to be present and unharmed."

"Thank Heavens!"

Viola awoke as a loud cheer went up and for a moment she did not know where she was. She looked first at her ruined dress and then up at the Earl, who was smiling down at her with eyes full of love.

"Darling, look. Everyone has come to meet us."

"Viola. *Viola!*"

Aunt Mary could not be restrained. She ran down to the water and stood there, her skirts soaking up the sea, waving her arms at the approaching boat.

"Do not worry," shouted the Earl. "*She is safe.*"

Viola tried to get up but found that her legs buckled beneath her. As the boat hit the beach, the Earl swept her up in his arms and brought her ashore.

"Aunt Mary," she cried weakly, as she ran to join her.

"Viola, I have been so terribly worried. You are dreadful for going off like that. Anything could have happened – you might have been killed."

"But she has not," said the Earl, gazing at Viola, "she is safe, albeit very tired and a little bruised. She will need some attention to her foot."

Aunt Mary looked down and gasped when she saw the bloody makeshift bandage.

"Duchess, please call for the doctor," she asked, almost fainting.

The Earl wasted no further time. He strode up the beach carrying Viola.

As they approached the house, he was surprised to see that Millicent was sitting outside in her carriage, her eyes were red and puffy and she appeared to have been crying for quite some time.

As she saw him coming towards the front door of the house with Viola in his arms, she wiped her face and alighted from her carriage.

Millicent hung at the back of the crowd as everyone surged indoors. Even she could see this was not the time or place to make a scene.

"Quick. Bring brandy for the men," ordered the Duchess, snapping her fingers at the footmen. "Charles, bring Viola into the rear drawing room, it will be more private in there and I will make sure that no guests disturb you."

Aunt Mary followed the Earl and Viola and a maid came and lit the oil lamps.

"You will be fine, darling," murmured the Earl, kissing Viola's hands. "The doctor will be here soon."

Just then, there was a soft knock at the door. Aunt Mary rose to answer it and was shocked to find Millicent standing there.

"I just wanted to make certain that Viola is going to be all right," she began, hesitantly. "And I want to apologise to the Earl."

Aunt Mary looked back at the Earl and he nodded.

"I will go outside and speak with her," he said. "Viola, darling, I will return shortly. There is just something I need to do."

Viola snuggled down under a blanket that had been thrown over her as they had entered the house. She was curious as to what the Earl was about to say to Millicent.

"The Earl has said that he loves me," whispered Viola to her aunt who stood at the door, listening.

"Ssh, dear. I am trying to hear what he is saying to Millicent."

Aunt Mary's eyesight may have been poor but she had the hearing of a bat.

"Well, goodness me," she exclaimed. "I do believe that the Earl has just told Millicent that he does not love her and that he intends to marry *you*, my darling."

Viola looked shocked.

"Are you certain, aunt? Please do not raise my hopes."

"Wait and see. Here he comes."

Aunt Mary hurried back to the sofa and sat down next to Viola.

They both looked up at the Earl expectantly.

He had a very grave expression on his face as he entered the room. In a quiet voice, he said,

"Lady Wakefield, would you mind if I spoke with Viola alone please?"

"Very well," replied Aunt Mary, giving Viola a knowing look. "I shall let you know when the doctor arrives."

She left the room, trailing her soggy skirts behind her. As the door closed, the Earl remained standing.

"Viola, I have just told Millicent that she has taken our friendship the wrong way," he began.

'Oh, no,' thought Viola, 'does he mean that I have misinterpreted what he has said? Did I imagine that he said he loved me?'

"I said that as I intended to marry you, I only wanted friendship from her and nothing more. And if she found that idea abhorrent, then I suggested to her that I would refrain from calling on her again."

"Marry me?" exclaimed Viola, sitting up, "*you want to marry me?*"

"Yes, my darling, of course. With all my heart I wish it and as soon as possible. I shall ask your uncle's permission this very night."

Viola felt the room spinning. The Earl wanted to marry her. She fell back into a swoon and he ran to her side.

"Darling!" he cried, taking her in his arms. "Are you all right?"

Viola blinked back the tears. She was so overwhelmed with joy that she felt as if she had touched Heaven itself.

The Earl leaned towards her and their lips met in a passionate kiss. Viola felt her heart surge with love and she realised that all she could ever want was to stay in his arms forever.

"Darling, say you will marry me?" whispered the Earl, as he caressed her face and her hair, "say yes, please"

"Yes, I will marry you," murmured Viola, as they fell into yet more kisses.

Their passion was interrupted by a sharp knock on the door.

The Earl moved apart from Viola and in a voice still hoarse with emotion, he called out,

"Come in."

Aunt Mary put her head around the door and smiled joyfully at the picture of happiness she saw on the sofa.

"The doctor is here."

"Please show him in at once."

The doctor entered with his bag and examined Viola thoroughly. The Earl tactfully stood with his back to the sofa whilst the examination was in progress, as he did not wish to leave Viola's side.

"You are a very lucky young lady," announced the doctor, as he cleaned the wound on Viola's foot and dressed it with a proper bandage. "A few days rest should see you up and about, but I forbid you to go riding."

"That will be a hardship for me," answered Viola, "as I love riding."

"You will do as the doctor orders," said the Earl, sternly. "If he says you are not to ride, then you must stay at home and rest. Besides, as we are to be married, I want you to be well enough to walk down the aisle!"

The doctor smiled to himself but made no comment.

"I will leave her in your good hands, my Lord," he said, as he left.

"I had no idea that you loved me," admitted Viola, as soon as the door closed, "I thought that it was Millicent you were attracted to."

"No, Millicent is just a friend, but I fear that we will be friends no longer. Her aunt is a savagely ambitious woman and sought to make a match with me, regardless of my own feelings. Lady Armitage is used to getting her own way and she will be most displeased. I noticed that she had left the ball by the time we returned."

"But Millicent stayed – "

"I believe she thought that I had simply lost my temper with her earlier. She also is unaccustomed to people not bending to her will. She believed that I would run to her arms the moment I returned."

"But you did not."

"No," answered the Earl, stroking Viola's face. "I did not because it is *you* I love."

"I do not think I will ever tire of hearing you say that to me," murmured Viola, "promise me that you will tell me you love me every day of our lives."

"I promise," said the Earl, kissing her hands gently.

Their reverie was interrupted by yet another knock on the door. The Earl laughed and went to answer it.

It was Aunt Mary again.

"Hugo has just returned and is most anxious to see you," she puffed excitedly.

"Viola, darling, I will return. Stay here and do not move an inch."

The Earl kissed the top of her head tenderly and swiftly took his leave.

"Aunt Mary," exclaimed Viola, "he *has* asked me to marry him!"

Aunt Mary embraced her and began to cry.

"Dearest, I am so thrilled. You are perfectly suited and I am very happy for you both. When will the wedding be?"

"As soon as Charles has asked Uncle Hugo for his permission."

"I hope then that it will be very soon."

Aunt Mary paused, as if deep in thought, and inched closer to Viola as if she had a secret to tell her.

"Dearest, this is the second wonderful news I have received in the last few days."

Viola gave her aunt a puzzled look.

"Why, what might the other piece of news be?"

"Your uncle would be most displeased if he knew that I had told you, but oh, I cannot keep it to myself."

"Aunt?" asked Viola, quizzically. "What is it? Pray tell me at once."

"Last night while you were in your room with Mirupa, Hugo came to me and handed me that photograph of your Mama that had been hidden in your room for so long. He said that he had realised since you had been staying with us, that he had been a fool. For years, he had carried a torch for your mother, but when he was in the midst of the fighting at Bhuj, he realised that I had been his one true love all along!"

"Aunt, I am so glad for you," replied Viola softly. "And the photograph?"

"He gave it to me so that I might either destroy it or display it. He said that the choice was mine and that he would be happy whatever I decided. He actually apologised to me for being so awful."

"Aunt Mary, this is wonderful."

"The important thing, Viola, is that he has assured me that it is me who he loves and that he isn't still pining for your Mama. Whilst he does indeed mourn her, I now know that I was wrong to believe that I was second best."

"Then it is good news *indeed,*" enthused Viola.

Just at that moment, Uncle Hugo burst into the room, his jacket torn and the marks of battle clearly on his face.

"Do not be alarmed," he boomed. "I am not hurt. There was a skirmish down on the Chitterdee Road that had to be taken care of. Viola, you will be pleased to hear that the spies who have been stealing my boxes have been apprehended."

"How?" she asked. "How could you know who they were?"

"I have had my suspicions for a while and when I took a party out to search for you after you disappeared from the ball, we were intercepted by a messenger who was on his way out to tell me that the chief suspects were gathered in a house in Mandavi. It would seem that they had taken advantage of the fact that we were all out enjoying ourselves and had called a meeting."

"And so, you made a detour to apprehend them?"

"Yes, we did. And by Jove, we got our man all right."

"He was known to you?"

"We have had him under surveillance for quite some time. I could not tell you or Mary as it was top secret. But he has been a slippery customer and we needed proof that he was in cahoots with the Russians. There were two of them at the meeting. We have now alerted the Royal Navy to catch their ship in the Gulf. With any luck, they will be sent packing back over the border."

Viola heaved a sigh of relief.

"Do you think that we have seen the last of the Russians?" she asked.

"For now, yes," he replied, "but this war of nerves has been going on for nearly a hundred years – I do not think that it will all be over so quickly."

A footman brought in some drinks for them, followed by the Earl. He seemed delighted to see Uncle Hugo and clapped him on the back with gusto.

"So, you have brought in the bounders?" he said, heartily.

"Rather!"

"Lord Wakefield, I have something I wish to ask you," said the Earl, "would you consent to me marrying Viola?"

Uncle Hugo's face filled with pride and he shook the Earl warmly by the hand.

"You do not have to ask me. Ask the young lady herself."

"She has already said *yes*."

"In that case, you have our blessing. Promise me that you will make her very happy and will love her twice as much as any man possibly could. Now, we will need to decide on the day. Viola, do not let me see you on your feet – it is nearly light and, as soon as it is, our carriage will be ready to take us home."

With that, he put his arm around his wife's waist and led her out of the room.

"Goodness. I do not think that I have ever seen my uncle so animated," exclaimed Viola, "tell me, darling Charles, did you know about my uncle's secret mission?"

The Earl nodded his head and smiled.

"Of course, but we could not divulge any information otherwise it would not have been secret. We have been watching these fellows for a long time, but we did not have the evidence to prove it. And then you came along and did it for us. Viola, if it were not for you, those spies would not now be behind bars."

Viola blushed and looked up at him coyly.

"Oh, I cannot believe it was all my doing. It was an accident that I happened across the boat in the cave. I did not go looking for it."

"Dearest, you must promise me that you will never do anything so foolish again. For a while, I thought I had lost you."

Viola looked up into his handsome face and her heart melted.

"Charles, I would do anything for you. I love you so much with all my heart and soul."

"And I love you too," replied the Earl. "More than my heart can tell you. I cannot wait until we are married and together. Our love is so strong that nothing or no one will tear us apart. I promise you this, Viola, I am yours until the end of time itself."

"Yes, for ever," she answered, as their lips met yet again.

Viola clung to the Earl as they embraced, knowing that she had found Heaven on earth and a love that would last for eternity.

"*For ever and ever –* " she murmured, love filling every inch of her soul.